MIND OVER MAGIC

by Stefan Petrucha

Penguin Young Readers Licenses
An Imprint of Penguin Random House

PENGUIN YOUNG READERS LICENSES
An Imprint of Penguin Random House LLC

Cover illustration by Patrick Spaziante.

ISBN 9781524787813   10 9 8 7 6 5 4 3 2 1

Chapter 1

The Angel Grove Youth Center was a bright, warm, inviting place. It had plenty of room for all sorts of activities, from karate classes and competitions to food drives and costume parties. Naturally, it was a big draw for teens from all over the city. And the Mighty Morphin Power Rangers were no exception. When they weren't busy trying to save the planet Earth from the evil sorceress Rita Repulsa or attending school, they often gathered there.

Right now, for instance, Tommy Oliver, secretly the Green Ranger, was standing on a practice mat and asking the Blue Ranger, Billy Cranston, to hit him.

"Come on, hit me," Tommy said. "You won't hurt me. That's why we're dressed this way."

It was true. Aside from the traditional karate uniforms, they both wore safety pads to prevent injuries. Remembering the stance Tommy had taught him, Billy positioned his feet and let loose with a palm-fist strike. It landed squarely on Tommy's padded arm. Tommy just waved Billy forward to try again.

"Again, harder!" Tommy said.

Billy, confused, looked at him. "I believe that *was* hard," he said.

Tommy shook his head. "I know you can do better," he whispered. "Pretend I'm Goldar. I'm about to destroy an orphanage, and you have to stop me!"

Billy frowned and said, "Goldar is Rita's second-in-command, winged, clearly simian, wears golden armor, and has crimson eyes. There really isn't any similarity."

The other rangers, all in their civilian clothes, watched from the sidelines.

Kimberly Ann Hart, the Pink Ranger, called out, "Billy, just pretend. We've been in hundreds of practice sessions."

"I realize that," Billy said. "It's just different from the simpler moves, and I like to think about things. It's not as if I've been doing it long enough to develop a body memory."

"Body memory?" Tommy asked.

When the others also seemed confused, Trini Kwan, the Yellow Ranger, explained, "It's when you practice something for so long, you can do it without thinking, as if your body remembers what to do." She eyed Billy. "But we're not here to talk, are we?"

With a shrug, Billy closed his eyes and let loose with another punch. As he did, Trini and the Black Ranger, Zack Taylor, martial artists in their own rights, imitated his move. The fun-loving Zack was dressed in a dark T-shirt and jeans, while the popular Trini wore the latest bright outfit. They couldn't be more different but when they moved, they did so in sync, with the same focus and accuracy. The hardworking Jason Lee Scott, the Red Ranger, was a karate instructor himself. With a backpack slung over one shoulder, Jason kept his eyes on Tommy.

As Billy's second blow was about to hit, Tommy put out his leg. Grabbing Billy's arm, he used the momentum to pull Billy over his leg and onto the mat, where he landed with a thud.

"Good!" Tommy said. He put out his hand, both to congratulate Billy and to help him up.

Billy grabbed the hand and rose to his feet, half-smiling. "I wasn't aware that winding up on the floor was considered a positive thing," he said. "I just don't know if I have the knack for this. You guys are the real martial artists, and Kimberly's a gymnast."

Tommy shook his head and said, "No knack? Are you kidding? I've been practicing for years, and you're already pushing me to my limits." He patted Billy on the back. "Trust me, this was just as much a workout for me as it was for you. Besides, as Trini told me once, it's not about winning, it's about the dignity and spirit with which you compete."

"You remembered!" Trini said cheerfully.

Tommy nodded and said, "I always try to remember good advice."

Jason stepped closer to the practice ring. As the leader of the Rangers, he was always quick to be supportive. "I couldn't agree more. Billy's not only doing great, but Tommy's an excellent teacher," he said.

"Yeah," Zack said. "I'm going to try to remember those moves you taught him." He delivered a few quick chops to the air, but then spun into a cool dance move that made the others laugh.

Kimberly raised an eyebrow. "For fighting monsters or for the dance floor?" she asked.

"Both," Zack said with a smile.

"So what do you think the hardest move is?" Jason asked Tommy.

Tommy thought about it. "For me? The double flying kick," he said. "The timing has to be perfect."

"Same for me," Jason said. "But it is a powerful strike."

Billy turned to Tommy. "I truly appreciate the assistance," he said. "I only wish I had some way to return the favor." His face brightened. "I know! I could instruct you in chess!"

Tommy wanted to be polite, but it was clear he didn't like the idea. "Uh . . . I don't know if I'm a chess-playing kind of guy," he said. "Besides, you already do plenty for me as a fellow Ranger."

"I used to feel the same way about any kind of fisticuffs, but being a Ranger made me realize that the mind and the body are equally important," Billy said. "Maybe you should give chess a try. After all, it can be useful to see things from another perspective."

"I'll . . . think about it," Tommy said.

As Tommy climbed out of the ring, Kimberly gave the white sleeve of his karate uniform a friendly tug.

"Uh . . . so . . . ," she said.

"Yes?" Tommy answered, a befuddled look on his face.

She'd been attracted to Tommy from the moment she saw him, not realizing at the time that he was fighting against them as the Green Ranger. When Kimberly found out Tommy was secretly their enemy, it had broken her heart. But he wasn't evil, really. Rita Repulsa's spells were forcing him to battle against the Rangers and his true nature. Since then, the Power Rangers had freed Tommy from Rita's magic, and now they all fought together on the side of good.

Still, between monster battles and schoolwork, there'd been little time for the two teens to socialize.

But maybe now was the time to make up for that?

A little flustered, Kimberly cleared her throat and said, "How about we get together later at the Juice Bar? All of us?"

Tommy smiled. "Sounds like a great idea," he answered. "I just want to head home first to shower and change."

Once he turned to leave, Kimberly leaned over to Trini and whispered in her ear, "That didn't sound awkward or anything, did it?"

Trini shook her head quickly. "No, no, not at all," she said. Seeing two familiar figures enter the gym, she added, "But speaking of awkward . . ."

Chapter 2

Farkas "Bulk" Bulkmier and Eugene "Skull" Skullovitch were big fans of the Power Rangers, but they were also known for bullying. Whenever they ran into the Rangers in their civilian clothes, they unknowingly called their heroes losers . . . or worse.

They didn't seem to be there to make trouble, though. Instead, Bulk cradled a black lapdog while Skull gently carried a puffy white cat. Strangely, each animal was dressed in a little version of the traditional karate uniform.

Surprised to see the two caring about anything other than themselves, the curious Rangers found themselves staring. Tommy even stopped on his way out to ask, "You have pets?"

Bulk stiffened defensively. "No, if it's any of your business," he said. "We're only taking care of them while my cousin's on vacation." He held out the dog and said, "This is Stinkerbell."

"This is Lady Fluff," Skull said.

"And before you ask," Bulk added, "no, we didn't name them."

Skull held out the cat for Kimberly to pet. As she did, she said, "Trust me, I wasn't going to ask. But they are cute!"

It wasn't much of a secret that Skull had a crush on Kimberly. She was never mean about it, of course, but she also always made it clear that the feeling wasn't mutual.

When she turned to pet Stinkerbell, Bulk pulled the dog away. "I don't want Stinkerbell distracted," he said. "We need them both in top fighting form."

Trini's face dropped. "You didn't dress them up like that to make them fight, did you?" she asked.

"No!" Bulk explained. "Not really. But we did spend the last hour training them to play-fight like martial artists."

Stifling a laugh, Tommy said, "A whole hour, huh?"

"Now we're going to record them as they engage in the rare art of Pet Fu," Bulk said. "When we post the video online, we'll become Internet millionaires!"

"That's not how it works," Zack said, but the bullies weren't listening. Instead, Bulk's eyes got big and round.

"Millionaires," Bulk repeated. Then he sneered at the teens. "We've got the gym reserved, so, out."

"No problem," Tommy said. "We were leaving, anyway."

Jason waved the others toward the exit, but not even their serious leader could resist pausing at the door for a look back. In fact, they all watched as Bulk sat Lady Fluff and Stinkerbell in the ring a few inches from each other.

"Start recording," Bulk told Skull.

Skull aimed his phone and gave Bulk a thumbs-up.

"This is going to be gold!" an excited Bulk said. "Lady Fluff, combat stance six! Stinkerbell, she's coming for you! Defend yourself!"

Lady Fluff didn't move at all, but Stinkerbell took a step closer and licked the cat's nose. Frustrated, Bulk lay down on the mat and put his head closer to the animals.

"Where's your fighting spirit?" he asked. "Your discipline?"

In response, Stinkerbell licked Bulk's nose.

"Hey," Skull said. "I got that on tape! Cute animal pictures get lots of hits. Should I upload it?"

The thought horrified Bulk. "Just erase it."

"Okay," Skull said. He stared at his phone. "One button deletes it, but the other puts it online. I'm not so sure which, but maybe it's this . . . ?"

Bulk scrambled to his feet. "Give me that!" he said, grabbing the phone. When he saw the screen, his face went white.

"No, no," he said. "It's uploading!"

Trying not to laugh, the Rangers looked at one another.

"Juice Bar in an hour?" Tommy said.

"Right," Kimberly answered.

Chapter 3

Far from Angel Grove, in the observation tower of the ancient Moon Palace, the evil sorceress Rita Repulsa had been listening in on her sworn enemies. Raising her head from her extreme long-range telescope, she swirled around, mocking the ideals the Power Rangers held dear.

"It's not about winning? Ha-ha-ha! Of *course* it is! It's *all* about winning, and the cheating and lying you use to do it!" she howled.

Just to make sure her minions were paying attention, she whirled toward them and asked, "Isn't that right?"

All Rita's minions were cowardly, but some more than others. The biggest coward was probably Squatt, a wide-eyed, blue-skinned alien who looked like a hobgoblin stuffed into a helmet and armor. Terrified of Rita, he immediately nodded, even though he didn't know what he was agreeing with.

"Yes! Yes!" he squealed.

The second-biggest coward was Baboo, a tall alien who looked sort of like a cross between a monkey and a vampire bat. Thoroughly evil, Baboo was also very creative. He was in charge of producing potions and other devices for Rita's wicked plans.

"Winning is the best!" he chimed in.

Next came Finster, a brilliant inventor who resembled a Scottish terrier. He was Rita's chief monster maker. "I agree!" he said. "If winning's not important, why does everyone keep score?"

Goldar was the least cowardly. Rita's second-in-command, he resembled a manticore, a fierce mythological creature with an eagle's wings and a lion's head. In Goldar's case, his sharp-toothed face looked more like a red-eyed gorilla. As a warrior, he fought the Power Rangers directly. His lack of cowardice didn't mean he'd go out of his way to disagree with Rita, though.

"I always rely on cheating and lying in *my* battles," Goldar said.

They all had lived in the Moon Palace ever since some visiting astronauts accidentally released them from a cramped space Dumpster. The wise sage

Zordon had trapped them there over ten thousand years ago. Rather than learn any sort of lesson while being stuck, the moment they were free, Rita had gone right back to trying to dominate the galaxy, starting with Earth.

Rita was usually either angry at her minions about something or amused with herself. Being amused at the moment, she went back to cackling.

"Ha-ah-ha-ha!" she laughed.

Seeing that the evil witch was in a good mood, Finster figured this might be the right time to give her some news.

"My most dastardly queen," Finster said. "I've finally managed to put a new head on the shoulders of one of my greatest monsters! Bones, reveal yourself!"

In a flash, a terrifying figure was standing by Finster's side—a skeletal monster who held a mighty sword and wore a matching red hat, string bow tie, and flowing cape.

The creature bowed, took off his head, and tipped it like a hat. In a deep, hollow voice, he said, "I am Bones, at your service."

Rita twisted her brow at Finster and said, "Didn't

those pathetic Power Rangers already blow up this bonehead?"

Wincing, Finster said, "True, but look! He's perfectly restored: able to turn invisible, as you've seen, shoot eye-blasts, jump long distances, detach his pieces, use each as a weapon, *and* summon Skeleton Warriors! I've got a triple batch of them all ready to go! And, if I say so myself, his new head is even better than the one the Rangers destroyed when they, uh . . . utterly defeated him."

Eager to get back to some monstering, Bones bowed again.

Finster waited for Rita to say something. When she didn't, he realized she'd stopped listening. Easily bored, she was back at her telescope. There, a glimpse of the handsome, noble, dark-haired Tommy Oliver totally soured her mood.

She shook her head so hard that her dual-horned hairdo wobbled.

"Tommy, Tommy, Tommy!" she moaned, her voice thick with disappointment. "Once you were my very own evil Green Ranger. I even gave you the Dragon Dagger so you could summon the Dragonzord! Now look at you, believing all that goody-two-shoes junk like helping your teammates and standing up for what you believe is right, with courage and discipline. Where did you go so wrong?"

Thinking he was being helpful, Baboo reminded her. "The Power Rangers broke your spells, your highness," he said. "You know, the ones that made him evil?"

Rita whirled toward him so quickly that Baboo and Squatt nearly fell over.

"That's not the point!" she screeched. "It was *my* Power Coin that gave the Green Ranger his powers in the first place, so *he* should be mine, too!"

Disappointed that she wasn't paying attention to his newly repaired monster, Finster again pointed at Bones. "It's rather a shame they can't just switch places, so you could give those powers to Bones here," he said. "He'd make an excellent evil Ranger, thanks to my . . ."

Rita raised a finger, warning Finster to quit talking. Her evil brain worked overtime. "What was that word you used? *Switch*? I think I'm having a great idea," she said. "Wait, it could be a headache. No, no, it's an idea! Didn't that foolish Blue Ranger create a mind-switching thingamajig a while ago?"

Squatt nodded. "Yeah! It was supposed to read minds, but I sneaked into his garage and messed with it, and he wound up swapping bodies with the Pink Ranger. Hee-hee. Sure was fun . . . until they beat us again . . ."

"Shut it!" Rita said, loud enough for Squatt to leap a foot off the ground.

Narrowing her evil eyes, she turned to the vampire bat-like Baboo and said, "Why don't *we* have one of those? Then I could switch Tommy with Bones and have my Green Ranger back!"

Baboo scratched his head. "Well . . . uh . . . ," he said. "I suppose if Squatt described what he saw, I might be able to copy it."

Already forgetting what he was shivering about, Squatt shrugged and said, "It was big."

"Big?" Baboo asked, hoping for more.

"Uh-huh." Squatt nodded cheerfully.

Baboo gestured in the air with his long claws, trying to get Squatt to say more. When Squatt looked confused, Baboo sighed and asked, "Can you remember anything else about it?"

Squatt scratched his head, his chin, and then his head again.

"Did I mention it was big?" he said.

Baboo looked nervously at Rita. "Uh . . . I think this is going to take a while," he said.

"I'll give you half an hour," she screamed, "then I'll burn you in oil!"

Squatt gasped and started talking. "It was about six feet tall, with space for two humans to stand in. In the middle, there was a thing with three buttons and a lever."

Baboo grabbed a piece of paper and started writing. "How many buttons did you say?" he asked.

Ignored again, Finster pouted. *Rita should have asked me to make the machine,* he thought. *Not that bumbling bat-face. Oh well, at least it'll be my monster leading us to victory!*

Sometime later, after a lot of questions and hard work, Baboo had a plan.

"I did it, I did it! Yes, indeedy!" Baboo said.

"And I helped!" Squatt chimed in.

"Give it here!" Rita commanded.

Baboo handed her what looked like a ray gun. But rather than one barrel, it had two, each pointing in a different direction.

More annoyed than curious, Rita eyed the two

barrels. "Why two? You think I can't aim? Is that it? That I'm nearsighted, like you salad brains?"

"No, no, your total greatness," Baboo said. "The Blue Ranger's machine was, well, as you heard Squatt say, *big*. The subjects had to get inside and hold hands. Thanks to *my* genius, I've shrunk it down to this convenient handheld size. Just aim the Mind-Swapper between two targets, pull the trigger, and the auto-sensors will lock on and switch their minds!"

Understanding, Rita stroked the Mind-Swapper with her long fingernails. "Not bad, not bad," she said. "Much better than your usual lamebrain failures."

"Thank you, I think," Baboo said. "Just one more thing . . ."

"It better be good!" Rita warned.

"Oh, it is!" Baboo said. "If the mind swap lasts long enough, a human victim will start to doubt whom they really are. Eventually, Tommy will start to think he really *is* Bones! Better still, it's not the same for a monster. Bones will always be Bones."

Rita was beside herself with joy. "Ha-ha-ha! Then I get my Green Ranger *and* Tommy back. Baboo, I'd kiss you if you weren't so ugly! Time to destroy the

Power Rangers once and for all!"

Baboo thought about mentioning how many times Rita had said those exact same words (forty-seven, he believed), but then he thought better of it and remained silent.

Chapter 4

Feeling good from his shower, Tommy strolled along on his way back to the Youth Center. What with the Power Rangers always teleporting here and there, he didn't always have time to appreciate the great weather. He was looking forward to the chance to sit and talk with his teammates, and not just because he liked their company.

Part of Tommy still felt terrible about all the evil things he'd done while under the influence of Rita. A smaller part worried that it might somehow happen again. The Power Rangers and Zordon had not only saved him, but they'd forgiven him and taken him in as one of their own. To this day, he looked forward to any opportunity to prove himself worthy of that trust.

He'd also gotten the impression that Kimberly liked him in more than a friendly, teammate way. Sometimes the same sort of feelings for her stirred in his heart, but Tommy wasn't sure what to do with them. Sharing some juice seemed the perfect place to start.

A few blocks from the Youth Center, he heard a strange noise coming from a dingy alley. It sounded like the wind chimes at his old dojo, but rather than being pleasant, this noise was awful, as if the chimes were made out of bones.

Plus, Tommy realized, *chimes can't make noise without wind, and there isn't any.*

Curious, he entered the alley, carefully scanning this way and that. After all the karate competitions he'd won, he was used to surprises in the ring. Being a Power Ranger had also taught him to be ready for anything *outside* the ring.

"Heads up!" someone with a slight British accent said.

The voice sounded bony, too: hollow and raspy. When the tall caped figure stepped into the light, Tommy understood why: It was a skeleton!

What could be keeping him together? Tommy wondered. Then he remembered Billy handing him a thick dossier packed with information about the monsters the Rangers had fought before he'd joined them. This skeleton was one of them.

At the time, Tommy had been a little impatient with all the long words and details Billy used, and he'd mostly read the dossier headings. Now he was grateful. Thanks to Billy, he had a good idea what to expect. Even so, he was surprised to actually *see* the monster remove his head and doff it like a hat.

"Let me introduce myself," the monster said. "I'm Bones, and you are out of luck!"

More skeletal creatures stepped from the darkness behind Bones. They were shorter, thinner, and all carrying smaller swords, but there were lots of them.

"I'm not afraid of you," Tommy said. Years of training had made him ready for a fight no matter the circumstance. But a Power Ranger would never strike the first blow, so he waited, ready to counter what they threw at him.

"How foolish!" Bones answered. But he didn't attack. Bones just crossed his bony arms, in a way that reminded Tommy of the skull and crossbones on a pirate flag, and stood there.

Tommy was about to use his wrist-communicator to alert the team when yet another figure emerged from the shadows. This one had a pointy hairdo and carried a crescent moon–tipped wand. Tommy would recognize her silhouette anywhere.

"Rita!" he said. "Whatever foul plan you've got, the Power Rangers will stop you, like we always do!"

"Is that a nice way to say hello to your first boss?" she asked with a grin. "I'm only here 'cause I missed ya! In fact, Tommy boy, I missed you so much I've come to take you back into the fold. Hear that? We're going to be together again!"

After a sharp cackle, she took a device from the folds of her cloak. As she fiddled with it, she said, "Just a sec . . . Now how the heck did Baboo say this darn thing worked?"

"I'd never join your side again, Rita," Tommy said. "No matter what you—"

Two thin orange rays shot from the device. One hit Tommy; the other hit Bones. As an orange haze covered them both, a cackling Rita said, "Yeah, yeah. Well, I'm not asking, I'm *taking*!"

The next moment, Tommy found himself turned around and in another part of the alley. Stranger still, someone else was standing where he'd been— someone who looked exactly like him!

"I don't know what kind of trick you're trying to pull," Tommy said. "But it won't work."

His voice sounded wrong. It was deeper, hollower, and had a slight British accent.

When he took a combat stance again, his body clicked all over. He looked at his hands. They were bones! He looked down. His body had become a skeleton!

No, not my body, he realized. *Somehow that ray put me in Bones's body! Does that mean . . .*

Tommy watched as the figure that looked like him tugged at its human head as if expecting it to come off.

Then he heard his own voice say, "Ah! This one's attached! I like it!"

It's true, Tommy thought. *Bones is in my body! I've got to warn everyone!*

He raised his wrist, but his communicator wasn't there.

Of course not, Tommy thought. *It's with my body! And so is my Power Coin. I've got to fix this.*

Tommy dove at Rita, planning to grab the Mind-Swapper. His movements were slow and clunky, and she easily teleported out of the way, reappearing deeper in the alley. There, she looked up, put two fingers into her mouth, and whistled.

"Quick, nitwit!" Rita commanded. "Before he

figures out how to use his new body!"

Squatt, sitting above on a fire escape, squealed as he tossed something round and black.

"Bombs away!" Squatt said.

It was only when it landed at his skeletal feet that Tommy realized it *was* a bomb. An instant later, it exploded!

Tommy didn't feel any pain, but the bony pieces of his body flew in all directions. His skull landed sideways against a garbage can, giving him a lopsided view of his arms, legs, and torso.

Bones could reassemble himself, but how do I do that? Tommy wondered. His limbs still felt as if they were part of him, as if he *should* be able to move them, but before he could try, Rita issued another command.

"Skeleton Warriors, you take your orders from me now!" the sorceress said. "Quickly, get him in those sacks!"

The skeletons each withdrew a brown sack. Tommy felt his parts being lifted and bagged, but he couldn't do a thing about it.

As one of the warriors picked up Tommy's head, he caught a glimpse of the sidewalk. There, a cheerful

Kimberly walked along, totally unaware of what was happening in the alley.

She must be on her way to the Juice Bar, Tommy thought. *I've got to warn her!*

"Kimber—*mmff*!" he said as his skull was stuffed into a sack.

All Tommy could see now was darkness, but he heard his own voice say, "One of the others is outside the alley. Shall I attack her?"

Rita snickered and said, "No, no! I've got a better idea. You're going to pretend to *be* Tommy and meet her. Then, when they least expect it, we'll destroy the putrid Power Rangers from within!"

"As you command," Bones answered.

Tommy could barely believe it. His worst nightmare was happening all over again. The Green Ranger was once again the enemy of the Power Rangers, even though it wasn't him!

Chapter 5

When Kimberly saw Tommy's familiar form emerge from the alley, her smile grew wider. Of course she had no clue that her teammate's body had been occupied by the mind of a monster.

Bones, not used to acting like a human, bowed stiffly and said, "Greetings, Kimberly Ann Hart. I am . . . Tommy."

Kimberly grinned and curtsied. "Uh . . . thank you, kind sir, but I already knew that!" she said. "I'm not used to you joking around. It's nice."

Unsure what she meant, Bones had to think about it. "A joke," he said. "Of course. Ha. It is good to laugh, is it not?"

"Sure is," she said, still smiling. "You're usually pretty serious."

When he didn't say anything, Kimberly worried she had offended him. "Not that there's anything wrong with being serious!" she added. "I really admire your discipline, actually."

"Thank you," Bones said. Thinking a human would return the compliment, he said, "And may I say that you have a fine head on your shoulders. Can it come off?"

Still thinking he was kidding around, Kimberly answered, "I hope not!" She nodded toward the Youth Center and said, "Juice Bar?"

"Is it?" Bones said.

"We're meeting with the others at the Youth Center, remember?" Kimberly asked.

"Of course," Bones said. "Where is my head?" He put his hands to his scalp and tried to twist it loose. "Ah, right here, of course! It doesn't seem loose or anything, does it?"

Kimberly patted him on the shoulder. "Uh, on second thought, maybe you should leave the jokes to Zack," she said. "Shall we get going?"

"Of course. I could use a drink," Bones said. "I'm bone-dry. I mean . . . I am very thirsty!"

The juice and gym area of the Youth Center was a wide-open space full of mats and exercise equipment. One wall had old-style coin-operated arcade games. The Juice Bar, operated by Ernie, provided a variety of tasty, healthy drinks. It was the perfect place for the Rangers. They could exercise, practice, and just hang out.

When Kimberly entered with Bones, she noticed that the others hadn't arrived yet.

Good, she thought. *It'll be nice to have some alone time with Tommy.*

But they weren't exactly alone. Bulk and Skull were also on their way in. Bulk was carrying Stinkerbell and Lady Fluff under his arms. Neither of the bullies looked very happy, until Skull spotted Kimberly. Then his face lit up and he came toward them.

Skull's big, goofy grin made his crush on Kimberly painfully clear. *I hope I'm not that obvious about my feelings for Tommy,* she thought.

"What happened to your Pet Fu shoot?" she asked, trying to be nice.

"Oh, we're taking a break," Skull said, "on account of Bulk got mad and caused a camera malfunction by throwing my phone against the wall."

Plodding along behind, a sullen Bulk said, "The stupid thing posted a . . . well, never mind what he posted."

Skull told them, anyway. "It was the cutest video

of Stinkerbell kissing his big nose," Skull said. "On the bright side, our video has more than one thousand hits!"

Annoyed, Bulk shoved Skull. "That is *not* the bright side, Skull!" he said.

Hearing the bully's nickname, Bones perked up.

"Skull, eh?" Bones said. "A fine name!"

Skull brightened at the compliment. "Thanks!" he said.

But Bulk and Kimberly both furrowed their brows.

Bulk nudged his sidekick in the ribs. "Don't thank him!" he warned. "He's one of them!"

"Oh, we probably have more in common than you think," Bones said.

Kimberly shook her head, as if she hadn't heard right. "Wait. What?" Turning to the bullies, she said, "Excuse us." Then she tugged Bones away.

As Skull watched them sit at a table, he fiddled with his phone, trying to get it to work.

"That Tommy's not so bad," he said.

Bulk made a face. "Cut it out. You're embarrassing yourself," he said.

"Hey, I fixed it!" Skull said happily. "And look, our video's up to one thousand five hundred and thirty-six hits! Talk about embarrassment!"

Seeing the look in Bulk's eyes, Skull backed up toward the exit. Bulk, who was still carrying Lady Fluff and Stinkerbell under his arms, stormed after him.

At the table, a worried Kimberly leaned in to talk with Bones.

"What were you saying back there?" she asked. "Skull and Bulk have been bullies for ages. Do you really think you have something in common with them?"

Bones shrugged. "They seem fine to me," he said. "I think that Skull fellow likes you. Maybe you should spend more time with him."

Confused, and now a little hurt, Kimberly sat back in her chair.

Is this Tommy's way of telling me he's not interested in me? she wondered. *Why else would he act this way?*

Chapter 6

With the pieces of his new skeleton body trapped in the darkness of separate sacks, Tommy didn't know what was going on. He didn't even realize Rita's minions had teleported him to the Moon Palace until he heard a loud, magical pop and Squatt said, "Gee, it's great to be back home in the Moon Palace!"

Tommy knew one thing, though: He had to escape.

If the Power Rangers think Bones is me, they'll treat him as a teammate. He could do incredible damage! Tommy thought. *This is as bad as when I was under Rita's influence!*

"Hurry, hurry," a fretful Baboo said. "That Green Ranger isn't just strong, he's crafty. I won't relax until we get all these sacks locked in a cell, especially with the Skeleton Warriors still on Earth with Rita!"

"Righty right!" Squatt answered.

Carrying all the sacks between them, the two picked up speed until they were practically running.

All the bouncing and shaking made the knot loosen on the sack holding Tommy's skull. To help it along, he rolled his head back and forth until, bit by bit, the knot came undone, giving him a view of torches, stone walls, and a curved stairwell heading down.

At least I can see, Tommy thought. *But my best chance at escaping is learning how to use this monster body before they lock me up.*

He was surprised to discover that moving his arms and legs really wasn't all that hard. Even though they were separate, they worked the same as if they were attached. At first, he had no idea which part of him was where, but by wriggling his fingers and toes, he quickly figured out which sack held what.

Baboo held the sacks with Tommy's head and torso. The bumbling Squatt carried the sacks with his arms and legs. Concentrating on his right hand, Tommy tried to untie the sack it was in. But this knot was tighter and if he moved too much, Squatt would notice.

While he kept at it, the bumbling minions reached the bottom of the long flight of stairs and entered a creepy stone hallway.

Guess this is the dungeon, Tommy thought. *Which*

means I'm running out of time!

He was right. Soon they stood before the iron bars of a rusty cell door. A fussy Baboo shifted the sack with Tommy's skull and unlocked the door. As it creaked open, Squatt kept his eyes on the door, giving Tommy the chance he needed to finish untying the knot.

The sack open, Tommy's skeletal arm sprang out. It quickly grabbed hold of the blueberry-colored creature's armor and crawled up toward his face!

Squatt screamed, "Yeow! It's got ahold of me! Help! Help!"

Dropping the other sacks, Squatt twisted this way and that, trying to shake off the arm. But Tommy held on tight.

Baboo was also startled, but he decided he had to prove he was at least braver than Squatt. He acted as if being grabbed by a disembodied arm was no big deal.

"Stop being such a scaredy-cat, Squatt!" he said.

When Squatt kept screaming, Baboo sighed and tossed the sacks into the cell, including the one with Tommy's skull.

"Omf!" Tommy said as his head landed.

Despite feeling each limb hit the hard ground, he focused on the hand clinging to Squatt. The skull now on the cell floor, Tommy wriggled it free from the sack, giving him an even better view of things.

Meanwhile, Baboo turned back to his squirming sidekick and said, "Here, let me give you a hand with that hand!"

He tried to catch the arm with his long, vampire bat-like hands, but the frightened Squatt was moving too fast.

"Hold still!" Baboo said.

"It tickles! And I'm scared!" Squatt complained. "I don't know whether to laugh or cry!"

"Will you stop being so silly?" Baboo replied. "After all, what can one arm do?"

But when Baboo got close enough, a bony fist gave him a good, solid punch.

"Oof!" Baboo said, staggering backward.

Punching Baboo meant Tommy had to let go of Squatt, so the arm clattered to the floor. Neither minion moved to grab it, though. Baboo was still stunned, while Squatt was furiously scratching the parts of his neck and face where the bony hand had been.

Seizing the opportunity, Tommy used the fingers to pull the arm toward the other sacks in the cell.

If I'm strong enough and fast enough, he thought,

I can untie all the bags and get out of here!

Seeing the arm inch along the floor, Baboo and Squatt cowered and started to argue.

Baboo tried to push Squatt toward it. "Hurry, Squatt!" he said. "Grab it before he gets the rest of himself free!"

"But it's so creepy! Why don't you do it?" Squatt said.

"It already punched me!" Baboo whined.

Tommy thought he might make it, when a new voice boomed along the hall, saying, "What's all the racket down there?"

Tommy turned his skull to see Goldar at the bottom of the stairs, shaking his head, annoyed.

"Don't you have the Green Ranger in that cell yet?" he asked.

Squatt and Baboo pointed to the crawling arm.

"Most of him," Baboo said.

"I'll handle this," Goldar said.

"Is that a joke?" Squatt asked. "Like *hand*-le?"

"I don't joke," Goldar said.

Tommy tried to make the arm crawl faster, but before he could reach the first sack, Goldar bent down and grabbed the arm.

Tommy tried to punch him, but it was no use.

"Not much of a fighter now, are you?" Goldar said. Feeling pretty superior, he tossed the arm into the cell with the rest of the bags. Then he clanked the door shut and locked it.

No! Tommy thought. Not about to give up, he started untying the sacks that held the rest of him.

Meanwhile, Goldar barked at Squatt and Baboo, "Get over here, you cowards!"

He grabbed the shaking minions by the scruffs of their necks. Yanking them toward the cell, he pushed them against the bars of the door and made them look.

Tommy's pieces were free now, but he couldn't control them all. They just flopped around, clicking against the stone.

"Look at that pathetic show!" Goldar said. "Is that what you're so afraid of?"

Baboo snickered. "When you put it that way," he said. "He is pretty pathetic, isn't he? He can't even make something of himself!"

"Yeah," Squatt added. "It sure is nice to make fun of him while we're safe and he's stuck behind those bars!"

Hoping to prove them wrong, Tommy rolled his

skull toward his torso. He tried to connect it to his neck, but it wouldn't stay put. The skull just rolled away, giving him an upside-down view of the laughing minions.

Just then, Rita Repulsa's voice filled the hall, sounding like fingernails on a chalkboard. Being an evil sorceress, she could call on her minions no matter where she was.

"Goldar!" she screeched. "Teleport down here to Earth now! I need a good warrior for the next part of my brilliant plan, but you're all I've got, you gold-chested ape!"

Goldar huffed at her insult then said, "Yes, your queenliness."

He spun and marched off.

Feeling safe, Baboo and Squatt lingered behind to keep making fun of their prisoner.

"You'd make a lousy monster!" Baboo said.

"Is that something I'm supposed to feel bad about?" Tommy asked. "You have no sense of loyalty, friendship, or love!"

"Oh yeah? If you think being human is so hot, just wait until we conquer your planet!" Baboo said. "Besides, knowing how to be a monster would certainly come in handy for you now, wouldn't it?"

As much as Tommy hated his new form, Baboo had a point. If he were going to fight back, he'd have to learn how to use this strange body. He started by trying to remember what else the Blue Ranger had told him about Bones. He knew that Bones had a few more tricks in his arsenal.

Didn't he say something about eye-blasts? he thought. *Yes, he did.*

Hoping to use that ability, the disciplined Tommy concentrated, putting all his energy into the skull, and then fixed his mind on the eyes. With a great effort, he sent two weak red beams sizzling into the hallway floor, right in front of Squatt and Baboo.

The flash and crackle weren't very powerful, but they made them both jump.

"Eep!" Baboo said. "Well, I'm sure he's secure in there. Besides, remember what I said to Rita earlier? If he stays in that body long enough, he'll start to think he *is* Bones. Then he won't be any trouble at all! And that only works on humans. Bones will always be Bones. We may as well go!"

"You got it!" Squatt answered, and they both scurried off.

Tommy's mind seized up. Was Baboo telling the truth about the mind swap? Could he actually forget who he was and believe he was Bones? If that was true, this was even worse than when he'd been under Rita's spell!

Chapter 7

Back at the Juice Bar, Kimberly tried not to stare at Tommy. This was partly because she was trying to understand her own feelings about him, but also because he'd been acting pretty strange.

Tommy certainly *looked* the same. Same hair, same face, same intense expression, same voice. Having said a few odd things, he was being quiet now. He was never very chatty, but this was more silence than usual. Whenever Kimberly talked, he just bobbed his head and stared off, as if he was waiting for something.

Plus, he hadn't touched his juice. Usually Tommy was pretty thirsty after a workout.

Maybe he drank a lot of water back at home, she wondered. But something told her that wasn't it.

"Don't you like your juice?" she asked. "I thought it was your favorite."

"Yes, of course. It is," Bones said. He picked up the

cup and took a long swig. "Ah. Delicious as always," he said.

But he didn't look as if he enjoyed it. To Kimberly, it looked more like he'd swallowed something awful and was trying to hide what he really thought.

She was about to come out and ask if anything was wrong when their wrist-communicators chirped. Invented by Billy, the communicators connected them to one another and to the Command Center. It was there that Zordon, their guide and mentor, monitored world events in case Rita attacked.

"Attention, Rangers," Zordon said. His steady booming voice was always calming, but he usually didn't contact them just to chat, so Kimberly listened intently.

"Goldar has appeared near the Youth Center and is causing a panic," Zordon said. "You've defeated him before, but this time there's something odd. Instead of the usual Putty Patrol, Goldar is being accompanied by the Skeleton Warriors once used by our old nemesis Bones!"

Hearing the name, Kimberly winced. "Bones?" she said. "But he was destroyed in another dimension when Trini threw his head into a lava pit!"

"I thought so as well," Zordon answered. "It's possible Finster repaired him. Be especially careful; you could be facing more than one foe!"

In the background, the excitable Alpha 5 issued his own warning. "Aye-yi-yi! Two at once! You'd better get over there quick!" he said.

"Tommy and I are on our way!" Kimberly said.

Through the communicator, she heard Jason say, "The rest of us are just a block away. It's Morphin Time!"

Kimberly was headed for the door when she noticed Tommy was hesitating.

"Come on, you heard Jason!" she said.

"Right!" Bones said.

With Bones following, Kimberly raced outside and found a quiet area in the parking lot. Once she was sure no one could see, she pulled out her Morpher, which contained her Power Coin. It looked a little like an oversize belt buckle, but it was much more than a coin or a buckle.

Left hand open, Kimberly held her coin in her right fist and called out the name of the prehistoric beast from which the coin drew its great energy:

"Pterodactyl!"

In a great, sizzling burst of light, Kimberly morphed into the Pink Ranger. Rather than street clothes, she stood in her proud, helmeted uniform and executed a few sharp jabs and kicks to test the strength, speed, and ability that the coin enhanced.

She looked to her side, expecting to see the Green Ranger. Instead, "Tommy" was still wearing his civilian clothes. She stared at him for a moment before he nodded sharply.

"Yes, of course," Bones said. Remembering what Rita had told him about the Rangers, he took out his Morpher and said, "Uh . . . Dragonzord!"

In a flash, he morphed into the Green Ranger. His practice moves were as sharp as ever, but the Pink Ranger still felt something was off about him. There was nothing she could do about it now, though.

Atop the large, wide Youth Center roof, Rita Repulsa sat on her bicycle, taking in everything the Pink Ranger and Bones said and did. Rita's bike was as alien as she was. It looked the same as any antique bicycle, with a huge front wheel and tiny back wheel. *Unlike* any other old-fashioned bicycle, hers could fly. And thanks to her magic, it carried Rita wherever she wanted to go.

Right now she wanted to be there, to see how her evil plan was working out.

Seeing the Pink Ranger run off alongside Bones made the witch grin. "It's working!" she said. Rita was so pleased, she wanted to cackle. But she didn't, lest she be heard.

Instead, she bit her tongue so hard it hurt.

"Ow!" she said. Then she leaned over in her seat for a better view and whispered to herself. "That puny pink teen doesn't suspect a thing! This will be even easier than I thought!"

Chapter 8

Peaceful and happy mere moments earlier, the scene in front of the Angel Grove Youth Center was now full of terrified people. They all screamed and raced in every direction to get away from the creatures that had appeared in the parking lot.

Goldar stood at the center of the panic, swinging his sword high above his head. A pack of Skeleton Warriors were at his back, hunched over and ready to strike.

His golden armor shimmered in the sunlight as the pug-faced fighter used his free hand to beat his chest like a mountain gorilla.

"Run, you silly humans, run!" he howled.

He swung the flat of his blade into a nearby trash can. With a horrible crash, it sent the heavy can skyward. It landed and rolled toward the fleeing crowd.

"You're not fleeing fast enough!" Goldar said, laughing at them.

The clacking Skeleton Warriors rushed toward the crowd.

Soon the monsters would be on them!

But they were far from unprotected. At about the same time, the Red, Yellow, Black, and Blue Power Rangers arrived. The Pink Ranger hurried in from the other side of the lot with the false Green Ranger beside her.

Seeing the endangered civilians, the Red Ranger knew exactly how to respond. Still running, he called, "Yellow and Black, get those people out of harm's way. The rest of us will hit Goldar and those Halloween rejects from both sides. If we're fast enough, we'll catch them right between us!"

"On it!" Yellow said. A series of cartwheels brought her near the struggling pedestrians well ahead of the skeletons. She took an older man's arm to help him up while the Black Ranger lifted a fallen child and brought her to her mother's arms.

Seeing the tears in the little girl's eyes, the Black Ranger said, "You're safe now!"

The girl sniffled, put on a brave smile, and said, "Thank you!"

Meanwhile, the Red, Blue, and Pink Rangers hit

the Skeleton Warriors, hard.

Red let loose a series of kicks and punches that sent two staggering. The Blue Ranger more than kept up, blocking a swinging sword with his forearm, then palm-fist striking the warrior's skull with the move the Green Ranger had taught him earlier.

The Pink Ranger grabbed a Skeleton Warrior by the shoulders, then twirled it into the air so it flew into two others. When another made the mistake of coming straight at her, Pink's high kick slammed it in the chin.

But where was the Green Ranger?

Whenever a Power Ranger took a breath and glanced around to see how the others were faring, the Green Ranger didn't seem to be doing much of anything. They all figured that he just happened to be catching his breath at the same time they were. Besides, between Goldar and all the Skeleton Warriors, there was too much going on to pay much attention to anything else.

It didn't seem to change things. The Red Ranger's strategy was working. Attacking from two sides had left the warriors disorganized and easy to pick off.

Watching from above, Rita chuckled. "That uppity

lunkhead Goldar is following my plan for a change, giving them a false sense of confidence before crushing them."

But when she realized the civilians were all safe and the Skeleton Warriors were scattering, the dastardly sorceress grew angry. As Goldar polished his sword, Rita cried out to him in that magic way only her minions could hear. "Hey, monkey muzzle! How can such a shiny helmet hold such a dim wit? I said a *false* sense of confidence, not the real thing! Look! They've practically won!"

Goldar glanced up and said, "Right. I'm so used to really fighting, it's tough to hold back!"

"So go! Fight! Just remember the Green Ranger is on *our* side!" she said. "I don't have to tell you which color uniform he's wearing, do I?"

With a nod, Goldar rushed into the fight.

"Leave Bones's . . . I mean, *my* Skeleton Warriors alone, you putrid Power Rangers!" he said.

Plowing into the middle of the battle, Goldar swung his blade in a long, wide arc that pushed the Rangers back.

The Red Ranger realized he had to adjust his strategy. "Green!" he said. "The others can handle the skeletons. You and I can take Goldar!"

Before the Red Ranger could reach him, Goldar vanished. At first he thought Goldar had fled, but then he saw that he'd only teleported to the far side of the huge parking lot.

"Come on, then!" Goldar called, beating his chest again. "I want you all to myself!"

Expecting the Green Ranger to be at his side, the Red Ranger raced toward his foe.

"Ha!" Goldar said. "Why did the Red Ranger cross the parking lot?"

Leaping into the air, the Red Ranger answered, "To get to the other side and defeat you?"

"Wrong! To meet your doom!" Goldar said, swinging his sword. "Hmm. I have to remember that one. I could use it again sometime!"

As Goldar finished his sentence, the Red Ranger dodged the slashing sword and forced both fists into the monster's chest plate.

The blow landed with a loud metallic ringing. It staggered Goldar, but he was far from finished.

When Goldar came at him again, the Red Ranger realized he was still alone.

"Green!" Red called. He jumped to avoid Goldar's

sword, barely making it, then looked for his friend and ally. The false Green Ranger was still all the way on the other side of the parking lot.

The Red Ranger shouted at him, "Some help?"

Bones waved and said, "Be right there!"

Hmm. Rita wants me to mess up the Rangers without revealing the mind swap, the villain thought. *This should be fun.*

He did head toward the Red Ranger but very, very slowly. Seeing a chance to cause more trouble, Bones stuck out his leg and tripped the Blue Ranger when he passed.

"What the . . . ?" Blue said as he fell, barely missing being struck by a skeletal sword.

Dazed, Blue didn't know what had tripped him, or notice Bones giving the warrior a little wink. Bones put a hand out, as if to help the Blue Ranger to his feet, then pulled it away at the last second.

"Oops!" Bones said. "It seems I'm all bones! I mean, thumbs. I'm all thumbs."

But the Blue Ranger simply rolled backward and flipped to standing. "Don't worry about it," Blue said. "I just used a move you taught me this morning."

"Uh . . . yes . . . you did. Good job!" Bones answered.

Meanwhile, the Black Ranger used a rapid series of punches to drive a Skeleton Warrior backward. The warrior dropped its sword, which clattered at Bones's feet.

"Green!" the Black Ranger said. "I set him up; you knock him down! Just like in practice!"

"Certainly," Bones said. But he thought, *That's not going to happen!*

Pretending to trip on the dropped sword, Bones kicked it right back into the Skeleton Warrior's hands. It was all Bones could do to keep from smiling as the Black Ranger had to duck the warrior's swing.

"What was that?" Black called to him. "I've never seen you stumble that badly before!"

Bones tapped his helmet, pretending he hadn't heard, and continued his slow walk toward Goldar and the Red Ranger. Along the way, he put himself between the Yellow Ranger and a skeleton she was about to strike, ruining her aim.

"Hey!" she said, but Bones ignored her.

Meanwhile, Goldar slashed and jabbed. But even without the Green Ranger's help, the Red Ranger was landing blow after blow. Rather than take Goldar down, though, the attacks only seemed to make the gorilla-monster even angrier.

"I will not let a human defeat me!" Goldar howled.

Swinging harder and harder, Goldar put Red on the defensive.

But when the Green Ranger finally arrived, the Red Ranger rallied.

"You mean *again*, don't you?" he said to Goldar. "We won last time, and we'll do it again, same as always, together!" Eyes on his foe, the Red Ranger spoke to Green, "I'll go high, you go low! Now!"

The Red Ranger went into a dazzling standing leap, kicking hard enough to knock Goldar's helmet half off.

Bones did go low, but not the way the Red Ranger expected. He went down on his hands and knees *behind* the Red Ranger.

When Goldar slammed him with the flat of his blade, normally Red would have kept his balance. This time he fell over the kneeling Bones and crashed into the asphalt.

"Ha!" a thrilled Goldar said. "If you're a martial artist, I'm a pastry chef!"

"What's up with you?" Red asked, thinking the Green Ranger had made a mistake.

"Maybe I'm coming down with something," Bones said. "I'm just not feeling like myself today. In fact, I feel chilled to the bone."

From somewhere above, Bones heard Rita laughing.

Chapter 9

Back in his cell at the Moon Palace, Tommy struggled to control the skeleton he'd been trapped inside. His teammates were in danger, and he couldn't just give up. No matter what he looked like, it wasn't part of who he was.

As long as I remember that, I'll keep fighting! he told himself.

Squirming and twitching, he worked to get each bone into roughly the right place.

It's not so hard, he thought. *It's like the old song. The head bone's connected to the neck bone, the neck bone's connected to the back bone.*

But even when the right parts were all next to one another, they wouldn't connect at all.

It's natural for Bones, he was created this way, Tommy thought. *But I just got here. I probably only managed those eye-blasts because of all my practice with the blade blaster. This is incredibly different. It's all about putting something together.*

He thought about other things he'd fit together in the past: models he'd built from kits as a young boy.

But those used glue or screws and nails, Tommy thought. *This is more like an act of will.*

Tommy had plenty of willpower but no idea how to use it here other than to keep trying.

What else has pieces? he thought. *Checkers and chess, but those pieces don't exactly fit together.*

Chess, though, reminded him of what Billy had said that morning: "Maybe you should give chess a try. After all, it can be useful to see things from another perspective."

Another perspective. Hmm. Maybe it would help to look at things as if I were Bones, he thought. *But how do I imagine a point of view I've never experienced? After all, I've never been a piece of something before.*

Then it came to him. *Wait . . . I have! The Power Rangers! I am a piece, a part of a team, and when we work together, we form something greater than any of us.*

Remembering their teamwork, honed by long hours of practice, Tommy tried to see the bones of his strange body as partners.

"Partners don't just command," he said. "They listen to one another."

Rather than ordering his body parts, he tried to sense what they felt. The bones didn't use words, but he could feel their urges and instincts, the way an empty stomach says it's time to eat. The moment Tommy tried following those urges, suddenly the bones all clicked into place!

As he stood, Bones's sword appeared in his hands.

Still feels weird to be a skeleton, Tommy thought. *But at least now I'm a walking skeleton, and I've got a weapon. Time to get out of here!*

The hinges on the door were rusted and weak. He could kick it down or use eye-blasts again, but that would make noise. Eager as he was to fight back, Tommy still wasn't in complete control of his body.

Going straight into combat might not be the best idea, at least not yet, he reasoned. *I should probably try not to attract attention.*

Planning to test the door, he stepped closer. When he did, his bony index finger seemed to have its own idea. Following the urge, he put it into the lock and turned. The door opened.

"Well, what do you know?" Tommy said to himself.

"It's like an actual skeleton key!"

As quietly as he could, he stepped into the hall and climbed the stairs. Reaching the next floor, he saw a long hallway. Billows of steam and loud noises poured from the only open door.

With a final hiss, the steam stopped, and Tommy heard a familiar voice.

"Excellent!" the voice said. "My Monster-Matic is in tip-top working shape!"

It's Finster, Tommy realized. *That must be the workshop where he creates all those monsters we have to fight.*

Part of him wanted to destroy the foul machine, but his first concern was warning his friends about Bones. While Finster hummed to himself, Tommy tried to sneak by. He had nearly made it, when his bony feet made a loud scrape against the stone floor.

Seeing Tommy, Finster howled, "The Green Ranger has escaped!"

For a second, Tommy froze. He could fight off the little dog-faced alien easily, but Finster might alert the others or create a Putty Patrol. Tommy could fight them, too, but the longer it took to get back to Earth, the longer the Rangers were in danger.

Remembering Billy's advice about different perspectives, he asked himself, *What would Bones do? Well, right now he's pretending to be me. Why don't I pretend to be him?*

"Green Ranger?" Tommy said. "No! I'm Bones, at your service!"

He tried to doff his head the way he'd seen the monster do. Surprisingly, it worked!

Finster's eyes went wide. "What?" he asked. "Are you saying the mind swap wore off?"

"Yes," Tommy said. "That's exactly what I'm saying. One minute I was in the Green Ranger's body doing . . . you know . . . evil. The next, I was locked up in a cell!"

Finster gave Tommy a closer look. Since it was Bones's body, though, there was nothing for him to see. Finster furrowed his brow.

"Can you prove who you are?" he asked.

Tommy thought. "Well, would the Green Ranger even be able to keep my bony body together or doff my head?" he asked.

Finster shook his head rapidly. "Of course he wouldn't. It *is* you! I knew it! Baboo isn't half the inventor I am. He must have done something wrong when he copied the Blue Ranger's device. This is great! No, wait, it's terrible! Oh dear."

It had worked! Finster believed Tommy really was Bones.

The minion grabbed what looked like a communicator and spoke into the mouthpiece.

"Goldar," he said. "Something's gone wrong with Baboo's silly Mind-Swapper! That's the real Green Ranger you're fighting, not Bones!"

With Finster focused elsewhere, Tommy slipped back into the hallway.

At least I've given the Rangers a fighting chance! Tommy thought. *Now I've just got to find a way back to Earth!*

Chapter 10

Back in the Youth Center parking lot, Goldar repeated Finster's warning: "That's the real Green Ranger?"

He looked at the figure he'd thought was Bones. Whomever was in that body had his back to Goldar and was very vulnerable to an attack.

It's just as well, Goldar thought. *Now I can prove I'm the best warrior there is by defeating both the Green and the Red Rangers!*

Growling, he leaned back and kicked the false Green Ranger from behind.

As Bones flew, he hissed at Goldar, "What are you doing, fool?"

"Kicking Green Ranger butt!" Goldar said.

The Red Ranger grabbed the flying Bones by the shoulders and spun sideways.

"You okay?" Red asked.

Confused and angry, Bones grunted, "Yes, thank you."

He wondered, *Whose side is Goldar on? It's not as if I can ask aloud! Perhaps if I get close enough, I can whisper without anyone else hearing?*

But getting closer wasn't possible with Goldar swinging his sword at them both!

"Defend yourselves, Rangers!" Goldar said. "Better yet . . . don't!"

Bones was so surprised, he didn't move. Rather than let him get hit, the Red Ranger pushed him out of the way.

Steadying Bones with a friendly hand, the Red Ranger said, "You should have seen that one coming a mile away. That must be some cold!"

"Oh, it is!" Bones answered. "Achoo!" he added, hoping it sounded like a real sneeze.

"Everyone! It's time to take our game up a notch!" the Red Ranger said. He raised his right hand and cried, "Power Sword!"

In a flash, a great broadsword with a gold-and-red hilt appeared. As the Red Ranger sliced the air, the Power Sword gave off an energy wave that shoved Goldar onto his back.

Following the Red Ranger's lead, the Black Ranger called out, "Power Axe!"

A quick thrust of his single-blade axe downed two Skeleton Warriors.

The Blue Ranger cried, "Power Lance!"

Spinning the tall double-bladed lance, Blue sent three Skeleton Warriors tumbling.

"Power Daggers!" said Yellow. Throwing the two short-bladed daggers had four warriors dashing into one another to get out of the way.

"Power Bow!" said the Pink Ranger.

When the glowing bow appeared in her hands, the Pink Ranger leaped. In midair, she fired a pink arrow that landed smack in the middle of a group of five Skeleton Warriors. When it exploded, they flew this way and that.

Not sure what to do, Bones stood motionless until Rita magically spoke to him.

"Dragon Dagger, doofus!" she whispered.

Nodding, Bones held up his hand and said, "Dragon Dagger, doofus!"

With a flash, the weapon appeared in his hands.

"Now make sure you use it *against* the Rangers!" Rita said.

Before he could, Bones found himself facing a group of his own Skeleton Warriors!

This is . . . ridiculous! he told himself.

Seeing no choice, Bones blocked their blows and ducked their swords. Being in a Ranger's body, he was shocked by how fast and strong he was.

When Bones used the Dragon Dagger to parry a thrust, he was surprised at the powerful pulse of green energy that sent the warrior soaring skyward. He was even more surprised when the warrior landed . . .

. . . right on top of Goldar!

Thinking Bones had done it on purpose, the Red Ranger saluted his teammate. "Nice aim!" he said.

The Red Ranger pressed forward with his Power Sword. When Goldar moved to counter, Red used a powerful circular parry that sent Goldar's sword out of his hand.

Bones gasped.

Despite his villainous efforts, the Rangers were winning! The Skeleton Warriors scattered, and the Blue and Yellow Rangers were rushing up to help fight Goldar. Seeing how suddenly the odds had shifted, Goldar scooped up his sword and turned to run.

Watching from above, Rita was completely furious.

"Aghh! What are you doing, you gorilla brain?" she shouted.

"Running!" Goldar explained. "Now that the mind swap has worn off, we're outnumbered!"

"What are you talking about?" Rita screeched. "The mind swap hasn't worn off! Who told you that?"

Still running, Goldar said, "Uh . . . Finster."

"Finster!" Rita howled.

Chapter 11

One of the things about being an evil intergalactic witch is that when you yell, your minions can hear you even if they're as far away as the Moon Palace. So when Rita howled, back in Finster's lab the screeching sound of his queen's voice made the alien inventor jump in fear.

"You dog-faced nincompoop!" she bayed. "Did you tell Goldar the mind swap wore off?"

Finster wasn't sure how to answer. Knowing Rita, it could be a trick question, but if so, what was the trick? Finally, he stammered, "Y-y-yes . . . yes, I did."

"Why?" she screeched, making him leap another foot.

"Because Bones told me he was back in his body!" Finster explained.

"He did, did he? And exactly why did that steam-baked brain of yours tell you it wasn't really the Green Ranger *pretending* to be Bones?" she asked.

"Because he had his body together and knew how to use it," Finster said. "By my calculations, that would take years for a human mind to learn."

Rita's voice grew louder. "Did you ever stop to think that maybe that ratty Ranger is smart for an idiot? Or that he's pigheaded enough to do that sort of thing? Which is why I picked him to be my evil Ranger in the first place!"

"Uh . . . no," Finster said.

"I'm getting a headache!" Rita shrieked. "Where is he now?"

"Why, he's right over . . ." Finster began. Then he realized Tommy was gone.

"Oh my," he said, quivering. "He was here a second ago, before you started screaming. He can't have gotten very far."

Finster was right about one thing: Tommy wasn't far. He was just down the hallway, hiding in the shadows. He'd been planning to search for a way back to Earth, but being in a monster body, Tommy could hear Rita, too.

I should listen in, he realized. *In case they reveal their plans or say something about how I can get out of here.*

But he couldn't quite make out Finster's fearful mumbling, so he had to get closer.

Carefully, Tommy lifted his head from his shoulders and rolled it along the floor. By sticking out his jaw, he stopped the skull outside the workshop door. Now he could hear and see everything.

"My headache is getting a headache!" Rita screamed.

"Oh dear, oh dear," Finster said, quaking.

A rush of footsteps made Finster breathe a sigh of relief. "That must be Bones now . . . I hope," he said.

Tommy was the opposite of relieved. Two shadowy figures were running full tilt toward the workshop. They'd spot his skull at any moment. If he tried to move it out of the way, they'd see that, too.

What do I do? I can't just run off without my head!

Then he remembered something else the Blue Ranger had said about Bones—he could turn *invisible*!

Great, Tommy thought. *Only how do I figure out how to turn invisible in one second?*

He tried imagining that no one could see him, hoping his body would understand. He couldn't see himself disappear, but somehow he sensed that it had worked—he was invisible!

The two runners certainly didn't see his skull. They almost tripped over it as they rushed into the workshop. But Tommy could see them. They were Squatt and Baboo.

Finster sighed. "You're not Bones *or* the Ranger!" he said. "What are you doing here?"

"We heard Rita screaming at you," Baboo said. "And, well, we wanted to watch!"

Finster's face dropped. "Oh you did, did you?" he said. "Well none of this would have happened if I hadn't suspected you of being a lousy inventor!"

Tommy realized he should put himself back together, in case he had to move fast. He crept closer to the door. His skull was invisible but, feeling around where he'd left it, he was able to lift it and put it back on. Tommy was practically in the workshop again, but no one could see him.

Not that the minions were paying attention to anything other than their bickering.

Baboo put his hands on his hips. "Me?" he huffed. "A lousy inventor? My Mind-Swapper worked perfectly. I demand an apology!"

"Grr," Finster said. "I'm sorry you're usually a lousy inventor!"

"Well!" Baboo said, pointing to the Monster-Matic. "At least the Power Rangers haven't defeated all *my* monsters!"

Above them, Rita shouted, "Aghhhh! The headache you're giving me is more powerful than anything either of you salad brains ever created!"

"Must be pretty big then," Squatt observed.

"Yes, *very* big," Finster said.

"Indeed," Baboo said.

"Shut up!" Rita barked. "The Skeleton Warriors are in retreat, and Goldar's teleporting back to the Moon Palace. But I've got an idea how to turn this to our advantage. We'll let the Power Rangers *think* the attack was just a diversion, that I have some really big plan in the works."

Baboo frowned. "But the attack *was* just a diversion," he said.

"And you do have a really big plan," Finster added.

"Ha-ha! That's why it'll be so *easy* to convince them!" she said.

Squatt frowned. "If you mean the big plan where Bones destroys them from the inside, didn't that just fail?" he asked.

Rita screamed again. "Don't remind me!" she

said. "Look, nitwits, as long as Bones is in the Green Ranger's body and those doofus do-gooders don't know it, I can have as many big plans as I want! And my new big plan won't be the big plan they think it is! Got it?"

The three minions scratched their heads.

"I think," Finster said.

Rita sighed. "Look, what's the first thing they do when they think I've got a big plan?" she asked.

"Beat us up?" Squatt asked.

They could all hear Rita's teeth grinding. "No! The *first* thing! First!" she said.

Finster rubbed his chin. "Try to figure out what your big plan is?" he offered.

"Yes!" Rita said. "And where do they do that?" Impatient, she answered the question herself. "In the Command Center, so they can get that fuddy-duddy Zordon's lame advice!"

"But sometimes they just talk to him with their communicators," Baboo said. "Maybe you should . . ."

Rita growled until Baboo fell silent. "We can sneak Bones a teleporter," she said, "so that once he is in the Command Center, he can teleport Goldar and the Skeleton Warriors in and attack!"

"Actually . . . that's pretty good!" Finster said.

But the still-invisible Tommy thought, *That's terrible! And I still have no idea how to get out of here!*

"I'll stay here on Earth to make sure Bones doesn't louse this up," Rita said. "The rest of you hollow heads, get to the throne room, fast! That's the only place in the Moon Palace with a teleporter that putrid green teen can use to escape!"

"Got it!" Finster, Squatt, and Baboo all said.

Got it! Tommy thought.

And they all raced for the throne room.

Chapter 12

Even though Goldar and the Skeleton Warriors had fled, the Rangers remained in the Youth Center parking lot. As they often did, they shared their thoughts on how to improve their skills and tactics. For Bones, the very idea of sharing was nerve-racking, especially since *he* was the subject!

"You seemed a little off at first, Green," the Red Ranger said.

"But you sure came through in the end," the Yellow Ranger added. "Blasting that Skeleton Warrior right on top of Goldar finished them off!"

In a supportive gesture, the Red Ranger grabbed Green's shoulder. "Absolutely," he said. "Don't get me wrong. That was a fantastic move, and it ended the fight. I just want to make sure you're okay. How's that cold you were talking about?"

Bones patted the Red Ranger's hand, then pulled it from his shoulder. "I am feeling better," he said.

As a creature forged in Finster's Monster-Matic, Bones only wanted one thing: to destroy whatever he was ordered to.

This camaraderie feels awful, Bones thought, wishing it would end. *But I must keep up appearances, no matter how hard it is, until I can convince them to visit the Command Center, so I can put Rita's plan into action!*

"Listen, my fellow Rangers," Bones said. "I feel that it's very important that we visit Zordon at the Command Center."

Puzzled, the Yellow Ranger tilted her head. "Why?" she asked. "He's probably hard at work with Alpha 5."

Hmm, Bones thought. *Humans care about one another. It's part of what makes them so weak. Maybe if I mention one of their foolish emotions, they'll respond.*

He turned to the group and said, "Well, you see, everyone, not having been there in a while, I sort of miss the old fellow. I am fond of him."

It did seem to have an effect.

"We're all fond of Zordon," the Red Ranger said.

"And Alpha 5," the Black Ranger added.

Everyone nodded in agreement.

"And, of course, Alpha 5. At the same time," the Red Ranger continued, "I'm sure that right now they're busy scanning all the available data to figure out what Rita's up to. If we had some solid new information, sure, we'd contact them immediately, just like they'll let us know the second they've got something. Otherwise, it would be irresponsible to interrupt them just to say hi."

This wasn't going as easily as Bones had hoped. Remembering the rest of Rita's instructions, he said, "But that's just it, don't you see? Rita *is* clearly up to something. I mean, Goldar showed up in the middle of Angel Grove with my . . . *the* Skeleton Warriors, and then we simply defeated them? It must be a distraction for some big, secret plan she's got in the works." For good measure, he added, "That evil, evil witch!"

"It *is* suspicious," the Blue Ranger agreed. "If Zordon was correct about Bones being resurrected, we do have to be especially careful."

That made Bones feel hopeful, until the Blue Ranger added, "But I do agree with Jason. There's no point in interrupting Zordon without more data."

"But . . . we *must* go to the Command Center!" Bones said.

This time it wasn't only the Yellow Ranger who was puzzled. They all tilted their heads and stared at the false Green Ranger.

After an uncomfortable silence, the Black Ranger asked, "Tommy, is this about when you were under Rita's control? Is that still bothering you? You know better than any of us that you can't live in the past. You're one of us now. Nothing's going to change that."

"Me? Worried about being under Rita's control?" Bones said. "No. Not at all."

In fact, Bones thought, *I rather like it that way.*

The Yellow Ranger crossed her arms and said, "I think it's more about that cold he's coming down with."

Bones latched onto the idea. "Yes, *that's* it. The cold," he said. "I thought I was better, but I am feeling *very* sick again. We should go to the Command Center and see if Zordon has some sort of cure for me."

There were more stares until the Pink Ranger said, "Cure? You mean, like . . . aspirin? I have some in my backpack that I can give you when we change back."

"That's a good idea," the Red Ranger said. "Things are quiet now. We may as well morph back to our civilian identities until we hear something."

"Hey, I could still go for some juice," the Black Ranger said.

Still trying to get them to the Command Center, Bones pointed at the Pink Ranger and said, "But . . . we already had juice."

The Pink Ranger shrugged. "I could use a muffin. Fighting always gives me an appetite."

As the others agreed and began cheerfully discussing what they would order, Bones gritted his teeth and thought, *No, no, no!*

Chapter 13

In the dank, twisty halls of the ancient Moon Palace, the still-invisible Tommy pushed his skeletal body to move faster. He was eager to find the throne room, where Rita had said a teleporter could be found, and use it to get to his friends.

Finster, Baboo, and Squatt were also on their way there, but Tommy had gotten pretty far ahead of them. As they fell farther and farther behind, he had a better idea.

They live here, so they'll know the fastest way, he thought. *I should be following them. As long as I'm careful, they won't even know I'm here until I'm gone!*

He slowed to a stop and waited until they trotted by.

"I felt something!" Baboo said. He nervously rubbed his arms. "Did you feel something?"

"Other than you stepping on my foot?" Finster huffed. "Not a thing!"

"Maybe it was a spider?" Squatt suggested.

"Ew! I hate bugs," Baboo said.

As the minions hurried, they kept stumbling into one another. Tommy followed, but left a lot of room ahead of him in case one actually fell.

Watching them huff and puff in their rush to obey Rita, Tommy couldn't help but laugh a little.

It would probably be easy to escape even if they did see me! he thought.

But another thought came to Tommy, one that didn't feel quite like his own. It felt like it came from somewhere else, a new little voice in the back of his head.

And it said, "Invisibility is fun! Being a monster isn't so bad, really!"

That worried him, especially given what Baboo had said about the mind swap making Tommy forget who he was.

Could that be it? Is this body trying to make me believe I am Bones? he thought.

Rather than stand around and worry, Tommy pushed the little voice aside. He had to stay focused on his goal: reaching the teleporter.

Up two curved flights of steps, they came to a wide hall with a high ceiling. It ended in a large archway.

Through it, Tommy could see an aged throne.

That must be it, he thought. *Now I just have to make sure I don't get caught while I'm looking for the teleporter.*

The stumblebum minions were in such a hurry to be first that when they reached the arch, they *did* trip over one another. Finster ran his furry hand along the floor then looked at the dirt it had gathered.

"I can see why Rita prefers to spend time up on the observation balcony," he said. "This place needs a good cleaning!"

"The Moon Palace was abandoned for thousands of years before we started using it," a gruff voice said from the shadows.

Oh well, Tommy thought. *And here I was hoping I'd only have these three stooges to deal with.*

It was Goldar, in a far corner of the large room. They hadn't seen him at first because there wasn't much light to make his armor sparkle. Sulking, his shoulders slumped, he paced in front of a small stone pedestal.

"Why are you here?" Baboo said. "Is Rita with you?"

"No. She's having too good a time watching Bones pretend to be the Green Ranger, but she didn't trust you idiots, so she sent me back to keep an eye on the teleporter," he said. He jutted his thumb at the stone pedestal behind him. "If it's as old as this place," he said, "I doubt it'll even work."

So that's the teleporter, Tommy thought. *Not that it'll do me much good with Goldar right in front of it.*

"And she trusts you?" Baboo said. Annoyed, he rose and stepped toward Goldar, nearly walking into Tommy on the way. "At least we didn't just lose to the Rangers."

Goldar said nothing, but from the way he winced, they could tell he felt cranky about the way the battle had gone. Baboo, Squatt, and Finster couldn't help but snicker.

"It is pretty funny that you couldn't beat the Green Ranger even when he was on your side!" Squatt said.

"Funny? FUNNY?" Goldar said, drawing his sword. "I'll show you funny!"

Squatt ran back toward the arch, shouting, "Yikes!"

Goldar sheathed his weapon. "If it had been the *real* Green Ranger, I *would* have beaten them. As it was, I only lost because of a stupid accident!" he said. "Now, why don't you lackeys make yourselves useful and search the rest of the palace for the prisoner you lost? I'll protect the teleporter."

Finster rose and said, "You can't order us around like that!"

"I not only can, I just did!" Goldar said. "I am second-in-command, remember?"

"Fine," Finster said. He grabbed Baboo's arm and tugged him toward the arch. "Come on," he said, "you take the west wing, and I'll take the east."

Baboo nodded, but then said, "You know, it's a pity we can't just wait a while. It won't be much longer before Tommy becomes convinced he *is* Bones!"

Tommy gasped. *That* was *what that little voice meant!* he thought. *How much time do I have left?*

All of a sudden, Finster froze and put out his arms.

"Sh!" he said. "Did you hear a gasp?"

Squatt, already back in the hall, rubbed his belly. "My stomach growled a little," he said.

Finster shook his head and said, "That wasn't it. Among the powers I gave Bones was the ability to turn invisible! I never dreamed that Ranger would figure out how to do it, but if he has . . ."

Fanning his arms, he started slowly moving toward where Tommy stood.

". . . he could be right here among us!" Baboo said.

"I prefer to finish my own sentences, if you don't mind!" Finster said.

Baboo turned up his nose and answered, "Then maybe you should talk faster!"

"Stop it, both of you!" Goldar said. "If he is here and he's invisible, we have to feel him out."

For several long minutes, the four searched the throne room. Fortunately for Tommy, being able to see exactly where they were made them easy to avoid.

If only Goldar would move farther from the teleporter, Tommy thought. *But he's probably the only one among them too smart for that.*

Indeed, Goldar never strayed more than a few feet from the pedestal. After a while, the frustrated minions gave up.

"Either he's not here or this isn't working," Baboo sighed. "Let's go check the rest of the palace."

Tommy exhaled.

But then Finster snapped his fingers. "Wait! I've got something that might work," he said. He reached into one of the many pockets on his smock and withdrew a handful of what looked like powdered gray chalk.

"Dust?" Baboo sniffed.

"Magic-clay dust," Finster corrected. "And here I was thinking of washing my smock. Good thing I didn't!"

He wandered, tossing the powder into the air.

Staring at the chalky clouds, Squatt asked, "Is it still magic?"

"Not particularly," Finster said. "But it doesn't have to be."

Realizing they might find him, Tommy headed for the hall.

Just before he made it, Squatt let loose with an incredibly loud, powerful "*Achoo!*"

The great sneeze sent a puff of the chalky dust right at Tommy, revealing his outline.

"Look!" Finster said.

As if the skeletal body knew the jig was up, it became fully visible.

Goldar brightened. "Great!" he said, drawing his sword. "Now I can defeat the real one!"

"Let's see you try," Tommy said, raising Bones's sword.

The two warriors came at each other, but as they moved, Tommy heard the others try to scurry away behind him.

"We've got to warn Rita!" Finster said.

Knowing that he had to stop them, Tommy instinctively sent his left arm flying away from the rest of his body. It swept along behind their legs, tripping all three minions.

"Aiee!" they cried as they fell to the stone floor.

As his arm flew back into place, Tommy thought, *I'm getting a little too good at using this body!*

And that little voice inside said, "Now, now! Don't say that! You can't be *too* good at anything!"

He tried to ignore the voice again. This time, it was a bit harder, and Goldar was still coming toward him.

"You won't find me as easy to defeat as those nitwits!" Goldar said.

Part of Tommy wanted to stay and fight. Part of his *body* was begging him to do just that. "Go ahead!" it said. "Show him who's the best!"

But knowing the Power Rangers needed him gave Tommy the strength to ignore it.

Much as I would like to defeat Goldar once and for all, getting back to the team is my first priority! Tommy thought. *And I'd better try not to use Bones's powers to do it. Otherwise, this body might get an even stronger hold on me.*

So he did something more familiar. Using his martial arts skills, he did a double flip that took him over Goldar's head.

As he sailed above the thuggish alien warrior, Tommy said, "Maybe some other time, Goldar!"

Still in midair, Tommy stretched out a bony hand and slammed it into a single ruby button that sat in the center of the pedestal.

Tommy disappeared so quickly, he didn't even hear Goldar cry out in rage. In a flash, he was standing in the parking lot of the Angel Grove Youth Center. He quickly spotted his fellow Rangers. They were on the far side of the lot, heading off. Their backs were to Tommy, so he shouted as loudly as he could to get their attention.

"Rangers!" Tommy screamed.

Instantly, they spun toward him.

But the hollow voice his friends had heard didn't belong to Tommy; it belonged to the body he was in.

I sound just like Bones! Tommy realized.

And, naturally, that's who the Rangers assumed he was.

"Zordon was right," the Red Ranger cried. "Bones is back!"

"No! Wait! Let me explain!" Tommy said.

Before Tommy could get out another word or lower the sword he still held in his hands, the true Bones, hiding in the body and uniform of the Green Ranger, said, "He's attacking! Stop him!"

And then the Mighty Morphin Power Rangers drew their blade blasters and aimed, unknowingly, at their own teammate!

Chapter 14

Weapons poised, the Power Rangers held their ground.

Tommy raised his skeleton hands and said, "Wait! It's me!"

Even as he spoke, he realized that saying "it's me" didn't exactly give his friends enough information, since he looked and sounded like Bones. As he was about to explain, the real Bones, in the Green Ranger's body, screamed, "Watch his arms! He's attacking! Fire blasters!"

The Power Rangers would never strike first, but they also trusted one another. Thinking the Green Ranger saw some weapon in Bones's hands that they did not, their fighting instincts kicked in and they let loose with a series of laser blasts.

Tommy's body also reacted instinctively, but not the way he hoped. His head, arms, legs, and torso all split off, moving out of the way in different directions.

No sooner did the pieces tumble than they lifted back into the air and reassembled.

Seeing the flying skeletal arms and legs, the Red Ranger said, "You're right! He's up to his old tricks!"

I've been in this body so long now, Tommy thought. *That happened automatically!*

That gave him two things to worry about. The first was that he might be losing his identity. The second was that the more he acted like Bones, the harder it would be to convince his teammates who he really was.

"We've got to destroy his head! It's the only thing that worked the first time!" the Pink Ranger said. She went into a series of cartwheels, planning to kick off Tommy's skull.

Oh no, not Kimberly, too! Tommy thought.

His body wanted to split apart again, to avoid getting kicked, but Tommy fought the urge. Instead, he somersaulted sideways.

"I'm not Bones!" he shouted. "I'm the Green Ranger!"

The Pink Ranger came out of her cartwheels, not sure she'd heard correctly.

"What?" she said.

The other Rangers also came to a halt, except the false Green Ranger, who held back, crossing his arms.

"How is that possible?" the Red Ranger asked.

"I don't know, exactly," Tommy said. "Rita hit me with some kind of ray gun. Finster said Baboo copied a mind-swapping machine that the Blue Ranger invented."

The Blue Ranger shook his head. "I did, but that doesn't make sense," he said. "My thought-transference device required that the subjects be inside the machine *and* touching each other."

Bones pointed at Tommy and said, "Don't you see? He's trying to fool us! If he were me, how could he split himself up and reassemble like that?"

Tommy gritted his teeth. "Because I'm in *your* body!" he said. "And you're in mine, Bones!"

"Liar!" Bones said, lying.

"You *have* been acting, well . . . odd," the Pink Ranger said.

"Because I have a cold!" Bones insisted.

Chapter 15

High above the tense scene, on the Youth Center roof, Rita was watching while perched on her bicycle. Lips curled in an angry snarl, she said to herself, "So, ol' Tommy boy thinks he can talk his way out of this, eh? I don't think so! Good thing Finster prepared that triple batch of Skeleton Warriors!"

Raising her wand, she aimed the crescent moon tip down into the parking lot. With a lightning-like crack and a swirl of curling smoke, the Rangers found themselves surrounded by dozens of the skeletal footmen.

"See that?" Bones said. "He summoned more Skeleton Warriors!"

"I did not!" Tommy objected.

"Then how did they get here?" Bones asked.

"You must have called them!" Tommy said.

But then several of the warriors aimed their swords at the false Green Ranger. Bones, confused that he was being attacked by his own minions, jumped backward, barely avoiding their attack.

"Wait. What?" he said.

Above, Rita cackled. "Sorry, bonehead, but I have to make it look good!" she said.

Understanding, Bones shouted to the other Power Rangers, "If I'm supposed to be controlling them, then why are they attacking me?"

With a rush of bony clicks, the skeleton horde swarmed forward, coming at everyone *except* Tommy.

"And why aren't they attacking *him*?" Bones said.

"He's right," the Red Ranger said. He fired at the closest skeletons.

The Blue and Black Rangers went back-to-back, dodging sword strikes and making counterblows.

"There are too many!" the Black Ranger said.

As Tommy watched his friends under attack, he thought, *I can't worry about who they think I am now; I've got to help!* He rushed toward the fray.

Seeing him, the Yellow Ranger said, "We've got to get to Bones. He's at the center of this!"

After blasting a group of warriors, the Pink Ranger had a clear shot at Bones.

I could summon my Power Bow and hit him from

here, she thought. *But Tommy has been acting so strange. It seems crazy to believe they switched bodies, but could it be true?*

Before the Pink Ranger could decide what to believe, she was shoved out of the way by the false Green Ranger!

"The rest of you deal with the warriors," Bones said. "I'll take care of that liar, Bones!"

Meanwhile, Tommy spotted two skeletons sneaking up behind the Red Ranger. Tommy was about to stop them, but a powerful blast at his back hurled him high into the air and across the parking lot.

As Tommy plummeted, he realized what had happened. *Bones hit me with my own weapon, the Dragon Dagger!* he thought.

He tried to curl into a ball to lessen the impact, like he'd learned in his training. But his body disobeyed. Instead, when he hit the ground, it broke apart.

Even faster than they had before, the parts reunited.

Tommy spun back around. The Rangers were up against a mass of Skeleton Warriors, but they were holding their own against incredible odds.

The false Green Ranger had left them behind,

though. He was racing toward Tommy, the Dragon Dagger out, ready to fire again.

It's like some weird dream, seeing myself running at me, Tommy thought. *But if another blast like that hits me, it's not going to feel like any dream. It's going to hurt.*

Tommy tried to plan a counter move, but his body had other ideas. His skull fired two eye-blasts that hit the false Green Ranger in the chest and threw him flat on his back.

"That's how you do it!" the little voice said.

A moment later, though, Bones was standing again. He gave his fellow Rangers in the distance a thumbs-up to tell them he was all right, then turned back to Tommy and laughed.

"Excellent," Bones said. "The more they see you use my powers, the more they'll be convinced I'm you!"

Worse, the little voice in Tommy's head was saying, "And soon, *you'll* be convinced, too!"

Chapter 16

The Rangers fought valiantly against the skeleton mob.

"Make a path!" the Red Ranger said. "We've got to help the Green Ranger take on Bones!"

The Pink Ranger, though, wasn't completely convinced what helping the Green Ranger meant. *I'll have to figure that out later,* she thought. *Whatever's going on, first we have to get past this skeleton crew!*

Surrounding the heroes, each skeleton linked an arm. Forming a bony wall, they struck at the Rangers with a circle of blades. The attacks were coming from all directions. The Pink Ranger couldn't see the Green Ranger or Bones anymore. It was all she could do to keep from being hit.

Across the parking lot, Tommy and Bones squared off. Bones shifted around, the Dragon Dagger in his right hand.

He's not even holding it the right way, Tommy

thought. *But he's so close that if a blast gets near me, it won't matter much. I could send my arms flying at him from opposite directions, use eye-blasts, or turn invisible and take him by surprise. But I don't want to do any of that. Bones was right. Using his powers would not only make it harder to convince the others who I am, but it makes it harder for me to stay in control.*

The very idea made a shiver run down Tommy's spine. Sure, it was a good idea to see things from other perspectives, but only to a point. If he was going to fight against his own body, he would do it as Tommy!

Hoping to take out Bones quickly, Tommy decided to try the most difficult karate strike he knew: the double flying kick. Concentrating, he readied himself, then waited for the right moment.

As Bones lifted the Dragon Dagger to aim another blast, Tommy came at him head on. Getting in close, he kicked his right knee up into Bones's abdomen. At the moment of contact, he pushed the knee down and used the force to bring himself into the air.

Finally, Tommy kicked with his left foot, slamming Bones in the chin with a loud, resounding THWACK!

Seeing this from the circle of Skeleton Warriors, the Red Ranger frowned and said, "Was that a double flying kick?" Before he could even think about what it meant, he was pushed back by the stabbing wall of warrior swords.

As for Bones, the Power Ranger helmet protected him, but he was still terribly stunned. Trying to keep his balance, he threw his hands out to his sides. That left him open for another strike. Seeing his chance, Tommy went into a series of hammer-fist strikes, one after the other. Still punching, he stepped forward as the moaning Bones was forced to move back.

"Aw!" the little voice said, disappointed. "You didn't use any of our cool powers!"

You got that right, Tommy answered.

Thinking the flurry of blows would finish Bones, Tommy began to feel better about his chances. But as he kept punching, he noticed that his skeleton arms were no longer connected to his body.

"Oh no! I'm using his powers without even realizing it!" Tommy said.

"Ha-ha!" the little voice said.

Tommy's surprise gave the real Bones the time he needed to let loose another Dragon Dagger blast. As Tommy flew back, he felt his body trying to come apart, but used his willpower to stay in one piece.

Not this time, Tommy told himself.

Slamming into the ground, Tommy shook off the pain.

"Ungh! Talk about other perspectives!" he said. "Now I know how my enemies feel when I use the Dragon Dagger against them!"

"That's not all you're going to feel!" Bones said as he fired another blast.

Still on the ground, Tommy rolled out of the way, but barely.

Chapter 17

Across the lot, trapped in the circle of Skeleton Warriors, the Pink Ranger had an idea.

"If we can't go through them, maybe we can go over them!" she called to the others.

"How do you mean?" the Yellow Ranger asked.

"Just give me a boost!" the Pink Ranger said.

Getting the idea, the Yellow and Black Rangers bent and cupped their hands. Putting a foot in their palms, the Pink Ranger grabbed their shoulders.

As her teammates lifted, she jumped!

A high-flying somersault took the Pink Ranger well over the heads and blades of the Skeleton Warriors. She hoped at least one other Ranger would be able to follow her, but instead the warriors rushed inward, tightening the circle in a full-press attack.

The Red Ranger kicked one in the chest while elbowing another behind him.

"We've got this!" he said to the Pink Ranger.

"You go now and help Green!"

"On it!" the Pink Ranger said and she ran across the lot.

As far as the Pink Ranger could tell, Bones was struggling to get to his feet. The Green Ranger was aiming the Dragon Dagger at him.

If that is the Green Ranger, the Pink Ranger thought, *it doesn't look as if he needs my help.*

But as she neared, she heard the Green Ranger say, "You're not only going to learn what the Dragon Dagger feels like, you're going to learn what it's like to lose!"

And then she heard the Green Ranger . . . laugh?

Bones barely made it to his feet. Wiping his skeletal chin, he took a shaky fighting stance. The stance looked strangely familiar to the Pink Ranger. She was even more familiar with what he said next:

"It's not about winning, it's about the dignity and spirit with which you compete."

That stopped the Pink Ranger in her tracks.

"You said that earlier today!" she said. "It *is* you in that body!"

Tommy was thrilled. "Yes!" he shouted.

The false Green Ranger only sneered. "So you've

figured it out, eh?" he said. "It doesn't matter. You see, I've figured out how to use this weapon's full strength!"

As he raised the Dragon Dagger to fire, the Pink Ranger leaped between them.

"Look out!" she cried.

"Pink, no!" Tommy said, but he was too late.

The Dragon Dagger blast caught her in midair. With a cascade of cracked cinder block and plasterboard, the force pushed the helpless Pink Ranger right through the wall of the Youth Center!

Chapter 18

Inside the Youth Center, hearing the raging battle, Bulk and Skull were trying to find a place to hide when a big piece of the wall came down with a terrible crash.

"Ahhh!" they both screamed.

Bulk scooped up the pets and hurried for the exit. When the dust cleared, they slowed down enough to look back. Seeing a pink-clad arm sticking out from the pile of wreckage, they both recognized the uniform immediately.

"It's one of the Power Rangers!" Bulk said. Afraid to get any closer, he leaned this way and that for a better look. "Is she unconscious?" he asked.

The Pink Ranger's fingers wriggled, and her hand began to feel around the fallen cinder blocks.

"Nope," Skull said. "She's just stuck. Should we help her?"

Bulk nodded at the animals in his arms. "I can't," he said. "I'm holding our whole cast. You go help her."

A frowning Skull asked, "Me? Why me?"

"Because . . . Ahhhhh!" Bulk said, his eyes growing wide.

"Ahhh?" Skull repeated. "What kind of reason is 'ahhh'?"

Bulk pointed. A skeletal figure in a cape and hat was coming through the hole.

"Oh!" Skull said, nodding. Then he screamed "ahhhhh!" as well.

Before the two could run, the false Green Ranger also clambered in through the hole. "Where do you think you're going?" he said.

Thinking he was talking to them, the terrified bullies froze. But zeroing in on the skeleton, the false Green Ranger slammed his helmeted head into its belly, making it break into pieces.

"G-g-guess he didn't m-mean us," Bulk stammered.

"G-g-g-g-good!" Skull said.

And they creeped toward the exit once more.

Tommy's body reassembled, but before he could move, Bones fired another Dragon Dagger blast that zapped him back into pieces.

Outside, the other Rangers were still trapped by

the scores of Skeleton Warriors. They hadn't heard what Bones or the Green Ranger had said, but that didn't stop them from seeing the Pink Ranger crash through the Youth Center wall. Concerned about their friends, they rallied.

"Pink and Green need our help, fast! Special weapons!" the Red Ranger commanded.

In turn, each raised their hands and called out their weapons' names, grabbing them as they appeared.

A downward swing from the Black Ranger's Power Axe sundered the skeleton circle. The Blue Ranger's thrusting Power Lance pushed the warriors farther apart, while the Red Ranger and the Yellow Ranger used their Power Sword and Power Daggers to batter the Skeleton Warriors repeatedly until they retreated.

"They'll be back," the Red Ranger said. "The only way to stop them permanently is to destroy Bones." He waved his arm toward the gaping hole in the Youth Center and cried, "This way!"

Chapter 19

From the roof, an excited Rita Repulsa watched them rush across the parking lot. When they climbed through the hole, though, she couldn't see them anymore. Twisting her head, she grew more and more frustrated.

"Oh, drat," she said. "I can't see what's going on!"

Inside, Bones saw the Power Rangers arrive. Rather than let Tommy tell them anything, he blasted him to pieces yet again.

"It was him!" the false Green Ranger said. "Bones used some sort of explosive to send Pink through that wall!"

"Odd," the Blue Ranger said. "Bones didn't use explosives during our previous encounter."

"Perhaps he used his amazing laser eyes?" Bones suggested.

Seeing the moving hand of the Pink Ranger sticking up from the debris, the Red Ranger said, "We'll figure that out later. Right now, Blue, you and the Black Ranger free the Pink Ranger. Yellow, we'll help Green take down that monster!"

"On it!" they all said.

"Let's all hit him at once," the Red Ranger said, as he and Yellow stepped up beside the Green Ranger.

"I couldn't agree more," the false Green Ranger said.

When Tommy had put himself back together once more, he again felt stuck in a nightmare. The Power Sword, Dragon Dagger, and Power Daggers were all aimed straight at him!

Outside, on the Youth Center roof, there was a flash as Rita and her bike teleported to a better spot.

"Fantastic!" she said, gloating. "Now I've got the perfect view for the final defeat of the pip-squeak Power Rangers! The only thing missing is . . . popcorn! Ha-ha-ha-ha!"

The high-powered special weapons hurtled at Tommy, his Dragon Dagger among them. Adrenaline pounded through his system. It made everything seem to slow down, but that didn't help; the strikes had been perfectly aimed. There was no place Tommy could duck, dive, or leap to, without being hit.

Though he hated the idea of relying on Bones's

abilities, he had no choice. Just before the weapons reached him, Tommy willed himself to fall apart, and then he became invisible.

"Yay!" the little voice inside him said.

As her Power Daggers sliced through the air, the Yellow Ranger said, "Huh? Where'd he go?"

"Don't you remember? He has the ability to turn invisible at will," the false Green Ranger said.

"That's pretty good," the Red Ranger said, retrieving his Power Sword. "Considering you've never even fought him."

Having seen Bones execute a double flying kick, the Red Ranger was suspicious, but not convinced. Many martial artists knew that move, but it wasn't Bones's style. In fact, they'd yet to face any monster who fought like that.

Bones worried he'd said too much until the Blue Ranger, while trying to uncover the half-buried Pink Ranger, spoke up. "I told him about Bones a few weeks ago," he said. "I was trying to catch him up on all the monsters we fought before he joined."

"How is she?" the Yellow Ranger asked, nodding at the Pink Ranger.

The Blue and Black Rangers had already removed

several of the heavy concrete chunks. The Pink Ranger used both arms to help, but her helmet was still buried.

"She seems fine. Our enhanced resilience and the uniform helped protect her," the Black Ranger said. "I think she's trying to tell us something, but her helmet-communicator's been damaged."

"Keep working," the Red Ranger said. "We'll fan out and try to find Bones."

He put out his arms and began walking slowly around the room.

"Watch your step," Bones told them. "He's a tricky one. Probably the fiercest monster we've ever fought."

"I don't know about that," the Yellow Ranger said. "But of course we'll be careful."

"Really?" Bones asked, feeling a little offended. "Who do you think was stronger?"

"Goldar, for one," the Yellow Ranger said.

"Goldar?" Bones said, stifling a laugh. "That piker?"

"Not now," the Red Ranger said. "Focus!"

As they searched, a few loose rocks trickled down the debris pile.

"There!" Bones said. Without another word, he fired the Dragon Dagger.

"Careful! You'll hit the others!" the Red Ranger warned.

Though Bones wished otherwise, the green energy didn't hit anyone. It did, though, raise a big cloud of concrete dust.

"Look at the dust!" the Yellow Ranger said, pointing. "You can see him! He's reassembled himself!"

A vague figure could be seen within the cloud.

Realizing he'd been spotted, Tommy put himself between the Pink Ranger and the others, then turned visible again.

This could be my last chance to convince them who I am, he thought.

But the little voice had grown stronger since he'd turned invisible. "What would you want to do that for?" it said. "Forget that silly hero stuff and just go with the flow!"

The Blue and Black Rangers crouched over the half-buried Pink Ranger, ready to protect her in case Bones dared to come closer.

But he didn't. Instead, Tommy said, "You've got to believe me! I *am* the Green Power Ranger!"

When the false Green Ranger moved to fire again, Tommy tensed.

The Red Ranger stopped him in his tracks, grabbing his wrist.

"Huh?" Bones said. "Let go of me!"

"No! Hold your fire!" the Red Ranger ordered. "You might hit one of us. Besides, I want to hear him out."

At those words, the air filled with a high-pitched squeal. It was coming from somewhere outside.

"Hear him out? No!" the voice said. "Don't do that! What are you waiting for? Fight! Fight!"

Tommy looked through the hole and saw a familiar robed figure on an overhanging section of the roof. She was bouncing up and down on an old-fashioned bicycle, shaking her fist.

"Rita!" Tommy said. "You did this! You swapped my mind with Bones's!"

As soon as he spoke, he realized the evil witch wouldn't just admit it.

In fact, without skipping a beat, she pretended Tommy *was* Bones.

"What're you talking about, Bonesy?" Rita said, smiling wickedly. "Such a big kidder, you wacky numbskull, you! Quit ribbing them. You know who you are!"

"You're Bones!" the little voice in Tommy's head said.

It was getting harder to ignore, but he steeled himself against it.

There's still a chance to turn the tables, Tommy thought. *The longer I keep Rita talking, the more likely she'll give something away. If nothing else, the others will realize I'm not her pawn.*

Tommy shouted back, "Confess, Rita! Tell them who I am!"

A sniggering Rita waved him off.

"Joke's over, bonehead," she said. "Go on, everyone, don't mind me! Fight!"

She's impatient, Tommy thought. *If I get her angry enough, the truth might slip out! But what would make her angry?*

Once again, Tommy tried to put himself in another's shoes, but imagining what it was like to be an evil egomaniac was particularly hard.

"Whose plan was it to switch my mind with Bones's, Rita?" Tommy shouted. "Finster's? Baboo's? You couldn't have come up with this all on your own; you're not smart enough!"

Even from this far away, he could see Rita's eyes

narrow and feel the anger well in her voice.

"Oh, you know better than that, Bones! All the good ideas are mine!" she said.

"Even this one?" Tommy asked.

Grunting, she hopped off the bike, clenched her fists, and paced.

"Oh-ho-ho!" she said, wagging a finger in the air. "You're trying to trick me, but it won't work! If I say the mind swap was *my* idea, that means there *was* a mind swap! But I'm not falling for it," she said. She tapped a long fingernail against the side of her conical hairdo. "Because I've got too much brain up here, Tommy boy!" she said.

"Wait!" the Black Ranger said. "Did she just call him Tommy?"

"Uh . . . no," Bones said. "I think she said mommy's boy. You know, like, a human insult."

"A *human* insult?" the Yellow Ranger said, staring at him.

Rita stomped her feet. "Bones! I meant Bones!" she said.

She spread her arms and screamed. "Aghhhh! Fine! But it *was* my idea, all of it! My idiot lackeys would lose their heads if they weren't attached, and in Bones's case, that's a big problem!"

At that precise moment, Lady Fluff chased Stinkerbell back into the gym. Bulk and Skull, huffing and puffing, appeared behind them, stopping short when they realized where they were.

"Agh! Did they have to run back here?" Skull whined.

Trying to stay out of the way, the bullies knelt and waved frantically at the pets.

"Stinkerbell!" Bulk said. "Heel!"

"Lady Fluff!" said Skull. "Please, come here! Pretty please?"

Meanwhile, the Rangers stared at Bones, Tommy, and Rita.

The Red Ranger slammed his fist into his palm. "It *is* true!" he said. "She switched their minds!"

"Whatever your plan is, you won't succeed," the Blue Ranger said.

"We'll stop you!" the Yellow Ranger added.

"Blah, blah, blah!" Rita said, rolling her wicked eyes. "Y'know, power punks, at this point, even *I* can't remember what my evil plan was! But don't you think for a second that means I've lost! Not as long as I have *this*!"

From the folds of her robes, she took out the Mind-Swapper.

"See how much you like your pals when you have to walk them!" Rita said.

Aiming at the Blue Ranger and Lady Fluff, she fired. Aiming at the Black Ranger and Stinkerbell, she fired again. Suddenly, the Blue Ranger was rolling on the ground, trying to lick his arms through his helmet. The Black Ranger got down on all fours and ran in a circle, as if chasing his tail.

The Rangers and the animals had swapped minds!

But Rita wasn't finished yet.

"And I think you two droolers have had all that power long enough!" she said to the Red and Yellow Rangers. "How about we give some other teens a turn?"

She fired, first at the Red Ranger and Bulk, then at Skull and the Yellow Ranger. In an instant, they had all swapped minds, too!

Chapter 20

Throughout the world, fans of the Mighty Morphin Power Rangers daydream about what it might be like to be Rangers themselves. As long as they realize it's a daydream, it can help them live up to the virtues the Rangers represent and be heroes in their own lives. But for the real Rangers, the wise sage Zordon selected a particular group of teens with attitude.

Skull and Bulk had an attitude, sure, but it wasn't the *right* attitude. While the bullies may have imagined being Power Rangers would be incredibly cool, the actual feeling of being zapped into someone else's body and suddenly given enhanced powers was pretty terrifying.

"I'm a Power Ranger!" Skull said, staring at his arms. "And I think I'm a girl!"

He looked up. His body was just a few feet away, looking just as confused as he was. "And . . . and . . . that's *me* over there, standing next to you!" He called to the person he thought was his friend, "Bulk, you've got to help me!"

But Bulk's form straightened and said, "I'm not Bulk, I'm Jas—uh, the Red Ranger!"

Meanwhile, the body of the Red Ranger, which was standing right next to Skull, said, "I . . . I think I'm over here, Skull!"

"Eep!" Skull said. "What are we going to do? Fight evil monsters? I don't want to fight evil monsters—they get giant!"

"I don't want to fight them even when they're small!" Bulk cried. "Let's get out of here!"

Bulk and Skull tried to run. Never having had enhanced strength and speed before, they slammed into each other very, very hard and wound up a tangled mess on the floor.

The bodies of Bulk and Skull, meanwhile, inhabited by the minds of the Red and Yellow Rangers, rushed up to defend Tommy.

The Red Ranger put his hand on Tommy's shoulder. "No matter whose bodies we're in," he said, "we're still Rangers inside, and we're with you!"

The Yellow Ranger glared at Bones and said, "You're going down!"

"Seriously?" Bones said. "Have you looked at yourselves? What do you think the three of you can do against me? Other than lose?"

He fired the Dragon Dagger at them.

Tommy's friends were no longer protected by uniforms or even their trained bodies. To protect them, he quickly separated his arms and tried to block the attack. Though he took the brunt of the damage, the Red and Yellow Rangers found their new bodies thrown backward.

As soon as they landed, the Red Ranger said, "Don't worry about us. It just takes a little getting used to!"

It was clear, though, that he was having trouble getting Bulk's body back on its feet.

But Tommy couldn't stop to help. Bones was running right at him. He went into a high kick that slammed into Tommy's jaw and knocked his skull off.

"Heads up!" Bones said.

The skull went flying, landing sideways on one of the arcade games across the room.

But the Yellow Ranger had some ideas of her own. While Bones was busy, she'd lifted a piece of broken mirror from the pile of debris.

"Green Ranger!" she shouted. "Eye-blasts!"

Tommy was torn. He was reluctant to use this body's powers, but it not only felt good to be called the Green Ranger again, he also trusted the Yellow Ranger—so he fired at the mirror. The Yellow Ranger held the glass at just the right angle so when the twin beams hit, they bounced off and hit Bones when he least expected it.

Knocked off his feet, Bones landed with a thud. The loud noise made Stinkerbell, who was in the body of the Black Ranger, yip loudly and race out on all fours. Hissing, Lady Fluff, now in the body of the Blue Ranger, followed.

Nearby, a terrified Skull and Bulk had finally untangled their Ranger bodies. Bulk, rising first, grabbed his friend's uniformed shoulders and pulled him up.

Deeply confused, he stared at the Yellow Ranger's body and said, "Skull, you're really in there?"

Skull nodded rapidly. "Maybe we're dreaming," he said. "And if we pinch ourselves, we'll wake up!"

Desperate, the two started frantically pinching each other's arms.

"It's no good," Skull said sadly. "I can't feel

anything through the uniform!"

"Keep trying," Bulk said.

But things for the Rangers were about to get much worse. Tommy's skull sat sideways on a pinball machine. He saw dozens of ominous shadows rising just outside the hole in the wall.

It's the Skeleton Warriors! he realized. *They've regrouped!*

Tommy began to reassemble his body, but the skeletons were already swarming in. As the pieces tried to fly together, some of the warriors grabbed his torso and arms, keeping them from reconnecting.

Scores more advanced on the Red and Yellow Rangers, swords out.

How can they even try to fight back in those bodies? Tommy worried.

But in the next instant, he learned that he'd underestimated his friends. Using one of their practiced strategies, the Red Ranger lifted the Yellow Ranger under her arms and swung her. As she kicked outward, a slew of skeletons fell back.

Strange as it was for Tommy to see Bulk's and Skull's bodies execute the maneuver, it made him realize that there really was more to being a Ranger than what was on the outside.

It's time I did my part, he thought. *Even if my parts are all over!*

Making his free leg hop along, he used it to kick the warriors that were holding his arm and torso until they let go. As soon as they did, he put himself back together.

"That's the way to do it, Bones!" the little voice inside him said.

Before Tommy could argue, Rita called to him from the rooftop.

"Come on, buddy!" she said. "Drop those losers and come back to my side! Sooner or later you'll be serving me again, anyway! Why wait when you can avoid the rush?"

Remembering the horror of being under her spell, he shouted at her, his voice full of defiance.

"Bones will never join your side again!" he said.

Tommy gulped. "I mean, the Green Ranger! The Green Ranger will never join your side again!" he said.

Had he been in the body too long?

Was Tommy forgetting who he really was?

Chapter 21

When Rita heard Tommy call himself Bones, she grinned so widely, her lips nearly cracked.

"Don't deny it!" she said. "It's happening! You know it; I know it! You're starting to think you *are* Bones! Pretty soon, all the Rangers will forget who they are!"

Eyes wide, the Yellow Ranger turned to Tommy.

"Is what she's saying true?" she asked in Skull's high-pitched voice. "Unless we change back, I'll start to believe that I'm . . . Eugene Skullovitch?"

Tommy nodded. "I heard Baboo say the same thing when they had me imprisoned at the Moon Palace," he said. "It's a side effect of the mind swap."

Even as he spoke, the little voice inside of him insisted, "You *are* Bones!"

No! I'm not! he thought.

"Are too!" the voice said.

"No!" Tommy said out loud, falling to his knees.

Seeing his struggle, the Yellow Ranger and the Red Ranger knelt at his side. They wanted desperately to help their friend, but weren't sure what they could do.

"We can't even ask Zordon for help!" the Red Ranger said. "Our communicators, our Power Coins, everything is with our original bodies!"

Bones scratched his helmet. "Hmm. This is most interesting. Does that mean I'll start to think I'm a Power Ranger?" he asked.

"No, numbskull!" Rita said, scowling. "It only happens to humans, not monsters! Now hurry up and attack those rotten Ranger teens while they're confused, or I'll start to think you're a *complete* idiot!"

"Of course," Bones said. Raising the Dragon Dagger, he went for them.

Seeing him coming, the Red Ranger said, "Remember, we're still Power Rangers!"

"Got it!" the Yellow Ranger said, nodding.

Rather than run away or hold their ground, they both raced at Bones, planning to meet his attack halfway, but the untrained bodies of Skull and Bulk were sluggish and difficult to move.

A charging Bones laughed at their bravado. "You

may be Rangers on the inside," he said. "But I'm bad to the bone!"

At the last instant, two pink-and-white gloved hands reached up from the debris and grabbed the ankle of the false Green Ranger.

"What?" Bones said. He went crashing forward, trying to kick himself free of the Pink Ranger's grip. But she held on tight, using the momentum of his fall to pull herself out.

Her helmet-communicator working again, the Pink Ranger said, "Trip or treat!"

Seeing the chance the Pink Ranger had given him, the Red Ranger leaped toward the fallen Bones. Bulk's heavy body landed flat on their foe, the weight forcing the air from his chest.

"Ungh!" Bones said, gasping. "And here . . . I'm not used to breathing . . . at all!"

As the false Green Ranger fought to get the Red Ranger off of him, the Yellow Ranger grabbed Bones's sword arm. Knowing the right pressure points, even in Skull's body, she was able to twist the arm hard enough to make Bones drop the Dragon Dagger.

"We haven't won yet," the Red Ranger said as he worked to keep Bones down. "I can't hold him for long like this, and more Skeleton Warriors are pouring in!"

Tommy was still on his knees, so the Yellow Ranger took his arm and tried to get him to his feet. "You've got to help us!" she said.

But Tommy was struggling and, it seemed, losing the battle.

"No, you don't!" the voice said. "Help Rita!"

"Who do I help? Who . . . am . . . I?" Tommy said.

Watching his pained efforts, the Pink Ranger immediately used her wrist-communicator to contact the Command Center.

"Zordon!" she said. "The Green Ranger is stuck in Bones's body and losing his identity. How can we help him?"

The ancient sage's voice responded calmly, as always, but didn't offer much hope.

"We have been watching, but there is nothing Alpha 5 and I can do from here," Zordon said. "I am proud that you all understand that being a Ranger is more about who you are inside than it is about power. I can feel Tommy fighting to remember that, but the effect of the mind swap is strong. He needs us now more than ever. The only chance is for you to help him hold on to who he is."

"I think I understand," the Pink Ranger said.

Dodging the oncoming Skeleton Warriors, she picked up the fallen Dragon Dagger and threw it.

It clattered to the floor in front of Tommy.

"Take it!" the Pink Ranger said. "It's yours!"

Tommy shook his head. "I can't use the Dragon Dagger!" he said. "It belongs to the Green Ranger! And I'm not . . ."

"You are!" the Pink Ranger said. "You are the Green Ranger! I believe in you, and I know you believe in yourself! I've seen it in a hundred fights. You just have to find that strength and use it!"

"Do it!" the Red Ranger said, as he fought to keep Bones pinned.

"We know you can!" the Yellow Ranger said.

Tommy looked up. Jason and Trini had the faces of Bulk and Skull, and he couldn't see Kimberly's face behind her helmet, but he felt the fierce friendship and loyalty in their voices.

If they believe in me, Tommy thought, *Who am I to give up?*

"No!" the little voice said. "You are Bones! Bones! It's time to conquer the humans!"

Bolstered by the faith of his teammates, Tommy said, "No one can tell me who I am. No one really knows, except for me and my friends!"

He picked up the Dragon Dagger and proudly stood, ready to fight.

Chapter 22

Tommy's first powerful swing created a green energy wave that knocked six Skeleton Warriors back out the gaping hole. Rather than use any of Bones's powers, Tommy executed a sweeping kick that sent even more clattering off their feet.

The little voice still objected, still wanted him to *be* a monster, but now he was fighting alongside his teammates. He could barely hear it.

He was Tommy Oliver, and no one, not even Rita, could change that anymore!

"Yes!" the Pink Ranger said. "Go, Green!"

Bones, meanwhile, managed to twist out from under the Red Ranger. The Red Ranger fell and had trouble getting Bulk's body to stand.

"You may as well stay down!" Bones said, laughing.

As Tommy rushed over to help, he blasted Bones, hurling him away.

"You're the one who should stay down," Tommy

said. "You've lost your strongest weapon, and now you're facing four Power Rangers!"

But the foul Rita, angry that the battle tide was turning, aimed the Mind-Swapper.

"I've had enough!" she said. "I'm going to switch that dratted Tommy teen with a mosquito, then swat him once and for all!"

In the precise instant before she could fire, a white cat leaped onto her face and dug its claws into her hair.

"Mmmf!" Rita said, her face covered by fur.

As she flailed, trying to grab the cat, Rita felt a sharp, pointed pain in her ankle. If the cat wasn't trouble enough, a small black dog was biting her!

Though trapped in the bodies of Stinkerbell and Lady Fluff, the Black and Blue Rangers hadn't run away. Instead, they'd sneaked up to the roof, unnoticed, to attack the malevolent Rita directly!

Rita half yanked the cat away, but the biting dog kept her tripping.

"What the . . . ?" she said. "Do you pesky pet Rangers really want a fight, or should I just drop you at a shelter?"

As Rita tried to shake the Black Ranger off her

ankle, the Blue Ranger bit her hand.

"Yeow!" Rita said, dropping the Mind-Swapper.

Before it hit the ground, the Black Ranger grabbed the Mind-Swapper between his teeth and ran off. Mission accomplished, the Blue Ranger followed.

"Get back here!" Rita cried.

Before she could reach the running animals, they hopped into a ventilation duct too small for the witch to follow and disappeared into the building.

"Meow!" the Blue Ranger said as they left Rita behind.

"Ruff, ruff!" the Black Ranger answered.

But each knew what the other meant.

"Ahhh!" Rita cried. "Now it's only a matter of time before those furry fugitives get everyone back in their original bodies! I won't lose again! I won't!"

A furious Rita ran to the roof's edge to check on the fight.

It was worse than she'd imagined. Tommy was aiming the Dragon Dagger at Bones. Since he was in a human body, a blast that close might knock him out completely.

"Oh no you don't!" she screeched.

In a last-ditch maneuver, Rita used her magic

to fire an energy blast. It careened toward Tommy. Instead of hitting him, the well-placed strike knocked the Dragon Dagger from his grip.

The mighty weapon went end over end until it landed back in the hands of Bones!

"Ha! No one aims like I do!" Rita said, gloating. Before the Rangers could react, she shouted, "Bonehead! Summon the Dragonzord!"

The Dragonzord was one of the Dinozords, amazing battle vehicles controlled by the Mighty Morphin Power Rangers that each linked to a powerful beast symbolizing their powers.

But Bones shrugged and asked, "How?"

"Do I have to spell out everything?" Rita screamed. She knew the Dragonzord particularly well, since Tommy had first used it when he was under her spell. "You have to play the Dragon Dagger like a flute!"

"Oh!" Bones said. He quickly played a tune, but nothing happened.

"Not that!" Rita yowled. "Don't you know anything about anything? How quickly you forget. It's a little number from the Zelton Galaxy, which I conquered thousands of years ago. It goes like this: da-da-dum-dee-dee-dee . . ."

Her croaky voice hummed the melody, and Bones repeated it.

Just off the coast of Angel Grove, a powerful rush of water churned from the ocean depths. The Dragonzord was on its way!

Chapter 23

Surrounded by a briny swell of twenty-foot waves, the Dragonzord burst to the surface. Reaching the Angel Grove docks in seconds, it flicked its sharp, drill-tipped tail, threw back its head, and let loose a terrible battle cry.

All the Dinozords were a sort of living machine. The others were based on the great dinosaurs that once dominated the Earth. The Dragonzord, though, was tied to something stronger: the wingless dragon.

Over 150 feet tall, the Dragonzord's two powerful legs carried it through the city streets. Its goal: to reach whomever held the Dragon Dagger. In the past, that had been Tommy. Now, unfortunately, it was Bones.

As the Dragonzord arrived at the Youth Center, all who saw it gasped and gawked. Rita's eyes twinkled with evil delight as her servant, in the Green Ranger's body, leaped toward the cockpit.

"Even lazybones can't mess this up!" she chuckled.

"Once he's inside, all he needs to control that Zord is the Dragon Dagger!"

But then her eyes nearly popped out of her head. Bones was not alone. The real Green Ranger was rushing up after him!

"I don't care whose body you're in or what weapons you have," Tommy said as he climbed. "You're not going to use the Dragonzord to cause any damage!"

"Oh no?" Bones said. "And just how do you think you can stop me?"

"Like this!" the true Green Ranger said.

Tommy wrapped his skeletal arms around Bones. They both landed on the Dragonzord's massive shoulder.

As soon as they did, Tommy sent a bony palm-fist strike toward his helmeted foe.

"And this!" he said.

But Bones twisted out of the way.

Of course, Tommy thought. *He's as fast as I am.*

Fighting against his own body wasn't the first weird sensation of the day for Tommy, and he wasn't about to let it distract him. When Bones karate-kicked him, rather than tumble, he stayed solidly on his feet and punched back.

As they grappled along the great, green metallic shoulder, Tommy unleashed a burst of kicks and punches. But Bones met and blocked each one. The instant Tommy paused, he found himself on the defensive, facing the same flurry of attacks he'd just used, but with the strength and speed of a Power Ranger behind them.

Thinking about his fighting techniques, Tommy found he could predict Bones's every move. Soon, it was Bones who struggled to keep up.

"I've still got one thing you don't have, Ranger," Bones said. "The Dragon Dagger!"

He sent a green blast hurtling at Tommy.

Tommy dodged, but the edge of the wide blast caught him, slamming him sideways onto the Dragonzord's hard shoulder. He saw the fight going on below, and it didn't look good.

The Red and Yellow Rangers were doing their best with Bulk's and Skull's bodies, but they couldn't summon their special weapons, let alone their Dinozords. That left it up to the Pink Ranger to keep most of the Skeleton Warriors at bay.

They're fighting bravely, but the numbers are overwhelming! Tommy thought.

But what Tommy couldn't see were the two animals, a cat and a dog, sitting in the shadow of the Dragonzord, both hard at work.

As the Black Ranger dog tried to hold the Mind-Swapper steady in its paws, the Blue Ranger cat used its claws to adjust the settings. Once done, the feline Blue Ranger meowed loudly, and the two struggled to aim the Mind-Swapper up, up, up at the wrestling figures above.

The short second Tommy had taken to worry about his friends had cost him. When he turned back, Bones was hovering over him, ready to bring the Dragon Dagger down for a crushing final blow. Even then, Tommy's thoughts weren't on the danger but on his teammates.

I can't let them down! he thought. But there was nowhere to go, no countermove he could think of that could possibly work.

"I'll knock your pieces so far apart, you'll have to take a plane to scratch your back!" Bones said.

Then they both found themselves bathed in an orange glow.

"Huh?" Bones said.

One second, Tommy was looking up at Bones, the

Dragon Dagger in the monster's hands. The next, he was standing, looking down at Bones, and the Dragon Dagger was in Tommy's hands.

In fact, they really were *his* hands. He was back in his body!

Bones, on his back, looked at his skeletal form, confused. "How did this happen?" he asked aloud. He looked back up to see the flat of the Dragon Dagger coming down at him.

"Uh-oh," Bones said.

THWAK! The Green Ranger swatted him. Bones slid across the Zord's shoulder and fell. Looking very small next to the giant Dragonzord, he tumbled down, down, down.

To avoid being hit by the falling Bones, a certain dog and cat had to scramble to get out of the way.

When Bones struck the ground, he broke into even more pieces than usual. Surrounded by puffs of rising concrete dust, the pained sound he made was loud, but not nearly as loud as Rita's scream.

"No!" she cried. "I'm not done yet! Get yourself together, now!"

As Bones obeyed, Rita raised her wand.

"I can hit a monster from the moon. You're so

close, Bonesy, I could do this one blindfolded!" she said.

Hurling the wand at him, she called out, "Magic wand, make my monster grow!"

It struck near Bones, surrounding him with a sorcerous glow. As the magic did its work, he started to grow, rising taller and taller, faster and faster. In moments, Bones was the same size as the Dragonzord, his giant shadow stretching all the way across the parking lot and into the gym.

Suddenly finding herself in Bones's shade, the Pink Ranger looked up.

"Wow," she said. "He must weigh a skele-ton!"

"No," the colossal creature answered. "I'm just big boned!"

Laughing hysterically at his joke, he lifted his enormous skeletal hand to swat the Green Ranger.

Chapter 24

Bones's gargantuan skeleton hand was definitely big enough to crush the Green Ranger. But Tommy dove into the Dragonzord cockpit just in time. The whole Zord shook as the blow slammed its shoulder. But the Green Ranger, keeping his balance, turned the Dragon Dagger sideways to use it as a controller.

The others are still in trouble, Tommy thought. *But right now, Bones is the bigger problem, literally!*

Bones's sword was now enormous as he drew it back to strike. Its tip nearly touched a tall building across the street, but before it came forward, Tommy raised both hands of the Dragonzord and fired a series of missiles from its fingertips.

Hissing through the air, all ten hit Bones. The explosions scattered his giant pieces. A huge arm landed atop six parked cars. A colossal leg splashed into the Youth Center's outdoor swimming pool.

Even Rita ducked, afraid she'd be hit. But the rest

landed in an enormous heap.

"Oh, my aching bones!" the great skull lamented.

As soon as Rita realized she wasn't hurt, she shouted at the disconnected collection, "Get up, you lazy Bones, and fight!"

Size made no difference. Just as before, the pieces briefly shook, rose, and reunited.

Bones glared at the Dragonzord. "I've got a bone to pick with you!" he declared.

He came forward swinging, but the Green Ranger commanded the Dragonzord to duck and counter. As the behemoths exchanged blow after blow, the citizens of Angel Grove felt the ground shake for blocks around.

Below, a smaller but equally important battle raged. Getting the hang of Bulk's body, the Red Ranger managed to palm-fist strike a Skeleton Warrior.

But there were a lot more where that one came from, and even more still streaming through the hole in the wall.

The only one who could summon her special weapon, the Pink Ranger, called out, "Power Bow!"

The moment it appeared above her head, she leaped up and grabbed it. Before her feet touched back down, she shot a flurry of pink projectiles at the warriors.

The explosions hit the front rank, tripping those behind them.

"Great shot!" the Yellow Ranger said in Skull's voice.

The Pink Ranger had to think a moment before answering, "Thanks!"

As she notched more arrows for another strike, she explained, "It's so . . . weird hearing you talk with that voice."

The Yellow Ranger shrugged. "Imagine how *I* feel!"

Nearby, the panicked bullies in Power Ranger form were again tangled on the floor.

"Unhook your hand from my arm!" Bulk said.

"Like this?" Skull asked.

The enhanced strength of Skull's Ranger body sent Bulk spinning and skittering away.

"Nooooooo!" Bulk said as he crashed against the wall.

Dazed, he heard a strange barking. "Yip! Yip!"

"Stinkerbell?" Bulk said.

But when he looked, he didn't see the dog. He saw the Black Ranger's body trotting up to him on all fours. He pressed his helmet against Bulk's hand and repeated, "Yip! Yip!"

"I think he wants you to pet him!" Skull said.

Bulk turned to see that the Blue Ranger's body was near Skull, purring.

Unable to take the craziness, Bulk closed his eyes. "Oh, please let me wake up, please let me wake up!" he said to himself.

When he opened his eyes again, he was briefly relieved to see Lady Fluff and Stinkerbell. Then he noticed they were aiming what looked like a laser pistol at him!

Bulk threw up his hands and begged, "Don't shoot!"

But the animals did, covering both Bulk and the Red Ranger in orange light.

Chapter 25

In a flash, Bulk was back in his body, but his problems were far from over because he was facing a Skeleton Warrior! As he turned to run, he saw the two pets fire again, this time at Skull and the Yellow Ranger.

The Red Ranger, now back in his body, immediately summoned his special weapon. "Power Sword!"

The Yellow Ranger called out, "Power Daggers!"

"Go, go, Power Rangers!" Red said, and they rushed to join Pink in the fight.

Now the dog fired at the cat and the Blue Ranger.

The first thing the Blue Ranger said when he was back in his body was, "Thanks! I think I was getting a hair ball!"

The dog, having trouble holding the Mind-Swapper on his own, yipped at him.

"Sorry, Black," the Blue Ranger said. "But it was crucial to restore everyone else first, since they were in the middle of a fight!"

He picked up the Mind-Swapper and used it on Stinkerbell and the Black Ranger.

"No worries," the Black Ranger said, exhaling. "But I am very happy to be back where I belong! That's everyone, right?"

As the Blue Ranger watched Bulk and Skull scoop up the cat and dog and run, he nodded, saying, "Affirmative."

Summoning their special weapons, they joined the fray.

"Power Lance!"

"Power Axe!"

Once the Skeleton Warriors were facing four fully powered Rangers, the tide quickly turned. Bones and swords scattered this way and that.

But above, the battle between Bones and the Dragonzord was at a standstill. Each giant was countering and returning one strike after another.

We've spent so much time in each other's bodies that we know each other too well, the Green Ranger thought. *Even when I land a solid strike, Bones just reassembles himself!*

Rita saw the problem, too. Now that the Skeleton Warriors were being routed, she was pretty unhappy.

"Bones," she said, "there must be something new in that empty head of yours!"

"Hmm," the giant Bones said. "How about this?"

He came at the Dragonzord, swinging the sword high above his head.

"Bone to be wild!" Bones said, laughing.

How is this new? Tommy wondered. *He's already done it a dozen times!*

Tommy got ready to block with the Dragonzord's arms, but Bones did have a new trick. Rather than complete his swing, he split apart!

The right arm continued the swing, which Tommy blocked. But the huge left arm flew behind the Dragonzord and smacked it in the back of the head. At the same time, the two great legs hopped to either side and kicked at the Dragonzord's knees!

As the Zord hopped around to keep its balance, the giant skull spun and floated up right in front of the Dragonzord.

"This time, you're finally going to lose. I can feel it in my bones!" the skull said. "No, scratch that, I can feel it in *your* bones! Ha-ha!"

"Really? Because I think you just made a big mistake!" the Green Ranger said back.

The Dragonzord grabbed the flying skull in its massive hands and held on tight.

"Let's see if you can get back together while I'm holding on to your head!" he added.

"What? Let go!" Bones cried.

He had his arms and feet punch and kick the Dragonzord, but Tommy did not let go.

Watching from below, the other Rangers rooted him on.

"Go, Green!" the Red Ranger said.

"Now that you have the head," the Yellow Ranger said, "you have to destroy it!"

"Okay . . . how?" the Green Ranger asked.

The Blue Ranger thought. "Last time we fought Bones, we used the high-intensity heat of a lava pit. Of course that *was* in another dimension," he said.

"Where are we going to get a lava pit in the middle of Angel Grove?" the Pink Ranger said.

Suddenly, Alpha 5's chirpy voice came through their communicators.

"Attention, Rangers! Zordon and I have been monitoring the battle and have found just the thing!" he said. "There's a partly active volcano seven hundred miles off the coast. It's not dangerous to the inhabitants, but the molten lava inside should be hot enough to destroy Bones. I'm sending the Green Ranger the coordinates."

"I don't think even the Dragonzord can kick that far!" the Green Ranger said.

Zordon's calm voice responded, "It is possible, but it will require a stronger connection to the Dragonzord than you've ever achieved before. I am confident you can do it, if you're sure of who you are again."

"I hear you, Zordon," the Green Ranger said. "And yes, I know who I am!"

Bones's arms were still punching and his legs were still kicking. But as much as the blows shook the cockpit, the Green Ranger managed to keep his grip on the monstrous head.

But can I do what comes next? he wondered.

Only the double flying kick could produce the sort of force he'd need. He'd mastered it as Tommy. He'd even done it in Bones's body. But he'd never even thought of trying it with the Dragonzord.

Zordon was right. The split-second timing would be twice as difficult using the controller. At the same time, Tommy had spent the day not only seeing things from other perspectives but finding his true self.

If ever there was a time he was prepared to try it, it was now.

Ready, he told himself.

The Dragonzord let Bones's skull drop. In the fraction of a second before it could fly off, the Green Ranger had the enormous living machine lean back on its tail for support, raise its knee, and kick. Using the momentum to lift the Dragonzord's body, he extended its second powerful leg until the heavy heel slammed into the skull, completing the second kick.

Bones's jaw flapped open long enough for him to say, "What the . . . ?"

Then his spinning head sailed off into the blue sky, swirling into the distance until it looked like a strange flying saucer.

The Green Ranger tracked it on the Dragonzord's radar. It hurtled along in a huge arc and finally came down, hundreds of miles away, smack into the center of the distant volcano!

Before the evil magic in the head dissipated, Bones screamed, "I should have quit while I wasn't just a head!" before being consumed by lava.

Back in Angel Grove, the rest of Bones's body

collapsed. The skeleton warriors, also exhausted, disappeared.

The Green Ranger exhaled with relief. He was happy to hear his friends cheering through his wrist-communicator, "You did it!"

"We did it," he corrected.

"You mean because I gave you the volcano coordinates, right?" Alpha 5 piped in.

"That, and the way you've all believed in me. In the end, it was the faith you had in me that pulled me through," the Green Ranger said. "Thanks."

"Well," the Red Ranger said, "you're welcome!"

Rita shook her wand and shouted, "I'll get you yet, you puny, punk Power twerps!"

In a burst of magical energy, she teleported back to the safety of the Moon Palace.

All that was left of her schemes was wreckage that could be easily repaired.

Chapter 26

A few days later, Tommy was standing outside the Angel Grove Youth Center. As he watched the masons finish patching the hole, a cheerful Kimberly strolled up beside him.

"Hard to believe the gym and juice bar are already back open, huh?" she said.

Tommy nodded, saying, "They're just doing some cleanup on the outside."

Before either could say another word, Bulk and Skull appeared, carrying Stinkerbell and Lady Fluff. The pets seemed fine. The bullies did not. They were looking around nervously, jumping at every shadow. Apparently they were still a little skittish after their mind-swapping experience.

All the same, Skull brightened when he saw Kimberly.

When they stepped up, Kimberly petted both the cat and the dog.

"They're not wearing their little costumes anymore," she noticed. "Have you given up on your Pet Fu project?"

"Actually," Bulk said. "we have a new idea. We're going to have them star in a horror film. It will make us rich."

Tommy frowned. "A horror film starring a cat and a dog?" he asked.

Bulk turned up his nose and said, "As if a loser like you could appreciate my artistic sensibility!"

Tommy stifled a grin. "Forgive me, but I *am* eager to learn, especially lately. What's it about?"

Though dubious, Bulk warmed to the attention. He put out his hands to paint a picture. "Well," he said, "in our new film, an innocent cat and dog fall prey to an evil scientist who switches their minds!"

Kimberly blinked and nudged Tommy. "That sounds familiar," she whispered.

"They say the best writers work from experience," Tommy whispered back.

"Yep!" Skull said. "There's only one problem."

"What's that?" Tommy asked.

"We have to teach Stinkerbell to meow and Lady Fluff to bark," Skull said.

Bulk slapped his friend's shoulder. "And it's not going to happen while we're standing outside chatting, is it? Come along!" he said.

As they went in, Kimberly called, "Good luck!"

Bulk kept his back to her, but Skull spun around long enough to wave and say, "Thanks."

"They're going to need it," Tommy muttered.

After hesitating a little, Kimberly turned back to Tommy. "We never did get together for juice," she said. "Well, I guess *I* did, but it wasn't exactly with you. If you're not doing anything, I could text the others to meet us. What do you say?"

Smiling, he shook his head. "Sorry, not today," he said. "I'm waiting for Billy. He's going to teach me chess."

"Really?" Kimberly said. "I thought that wasn't your kind of game."

Tommy shrugged. "It's not," he said. "But everything I went through really showed me how valuable it is to see from new perspectives. I figured, why not give it a try?"

"Good for you," Kimberly said. "Mind if I watch?"

"Only if you promise not to laugh when I lose!" Tommy said with a smile.

"Never!" she said. Leaning in closer, she whispered, "After all, Rita and Bones were defeated, thanks to you!"

He shrugged and said, "Like I said before, it's really thanks to the Power Rangers. We're all part of something bigger than ourselves. A team."

She smiled and nodded. "That's something I don't think Rita will ever be able to understand," she said.

At the same moment, far off in the Moon Palace, Rita was pointing at Finster, Baboo, Squatt, and Goldar, shouting at each, "Our defeat was your fault! And *your* fault! And *your* fault! And *your* fault!"

Rather than anger her further, her minions were forced to agree.

"Yes, your highness!" they said in unison.

And though the minions had never even tried to see things from another perspective, they were all thinking the same thing: *I hope she gets tired eventually.*